The Fearless Woman

M.L. Lexi

Titles by M.L. Lexi

The Blind Woman
The Deceitful Woman
The Forgiving Woman
The Grieving Woman
The Guilty Woman
The Loyal Woman
The Noble Woman
The Resolute Woman
The Unfaithful Woman

The Farfalla Family Saga

The Determined Woman
The Persevering Woman
The Invincible Woman

The Fearless Woman Series

The Fearless Woman
The Naïve Woman

Copyright

To family here and far.

Only when we are no longer afraid do we begin to live.

—Dorothy Thompson

Prologue

EVERYONE LIVES WITH the unspoken understanding of their obsoleteness. Still, you're never ready when it becomes your reality.

The idea that the inward comfort derived from a job Olivia had devoted twenty-five years of her life could be snatched away overnight made the anger spring hot inside her. Olivia cast enraged blue eyes to the email and reread it. The email from Catherine Sullivan, the president of Sullivan Foods, contained six lines of diplomatically correct legalese and the tenor of a sacking. Six aloof lines on an email were the sum of Olivia's years of commitment and loyalty to Catherine Sullivan.

Olivia's anger hot and pulsing, she bolted from the couch and paced the living room. Oreo, Olivia's black and white Maltese Shih Tzu, followed suit.

"Twenty-five fucking years I gave her. I worked nights and weekends without compensation. I never took a sick day, ever. I gave Catherine all I had, all of me, only to be fired over an email. She didn't even have the guts to say it to my face." Olivia's voice trembled with rage, and she increased her pace. Oreo withdrew to the couch. Comfort over exercise.

Olivia never saw it coming, but she blamed no one but herself for her employer sending her packing after years of loyal service. Deluding herself to believe that devoting her time, effort, heart and soul to her job would lead her employer to recognize her contribution rather than push her out the door was her mistake.

The boomer mentality of loyalty to your employer ingrained from a young age was corporate propaganda from institutions extorting a surplus of people seeking employment. Olivia knew that now, but it was too little too late.

Wisdom came at great cost.

There had been many little warning bells leading to this moment that Olivia chose to overlook for the sake of a much needed paycheque. The first overlooked red flag was when Catherine, the woman she looked up to and respected, knocked Olivia's salary by four thousand dollars. Catherine did so without explanation or cause at a vulnerable time in Olivia's life, knowing Olivia wouldn't contest it.

Olivia's nasty divorce left her in debt and desperate for money, and she couldn't afford to dispute the pay cut.

The second overlooked warning signal was when Catherine failed to pay Olivia the commission she'd worked for months to get. Again, Olivia did nothing. Financial insecurity leads to compliance, and Catherine knew it.

What Catherine did was beyond the pale and fundamentally dishonest. Still, Catherine continued to take advantage of Olivia, and Olivia had no choice but to allow it. Losing her home and not eating wasn't an option.

The hard-learned survival lessons taught Olivia that life was inherently unfair and pride was a commodity when debts were mounting.

Olivia had Bob to thank for the poor state of her finances. After ten years of marriage to Bob Huntley, he walked out on their marriage and left Olivia with more debt than she imagined one person could accrue. Marital debt, they called it, when Bob disappeared into thin air, and Olivia was on the hook for the entire amount. Never mind that Bob had forged her signature on the credit card applications or the second mortgage documents and cleaned out their bank accounts.

It took Olivia years to pay off the debt she was left to shoulder and just as long to gain her financial footing. With the debt paid, the massive boulder on her shoulders slid away. Olivia had never felt as free or as secure as she did then.

Independence accomplished, Olivia shed Bob's surname and reclaimed her maiden name. Falco wasn't regal or a legacy name, but it was hers, and Olivia Huntley became Olivia Falco.

Under the name Olivia Falco, she opened bank and investment accounts. Managing her money, bank accounts, and investments, something Bob didn't allow during their marriage, felt liberating.

Bob had controlled their finances and purposely kept Olivia in the dark during their marriage. It wasn't until Bob left that Olivia discovered he was as bad a money manager as he was a husband. It wasn't until then she went over the credit card statements and saw the gambling charges. It wasn't until then she saw the motel charges and, on deeper detecting, found out he was "entertaining" a parade of women.

Aside from trusting Bob and leaving him in charge of their finances, marrying him was something Olivia would regret all her life.

But there was a silver lining to every dark cloud. Olivia's cheating, lying husband helped her recognize her inner strength and self-reliance. That knowledge gave Olivia control over her life, the money she never had with Bob, and a taste of independence. It tasted great, and keeping her newfound freedom was a powerful motivator for Olivia to do everything necessary to maintain it.

Olivia gave everything she had to her job and the company that helped make it possible to get her life in order. She walked the line and did what was asked of her. She went above and beyond because she was grateful, loved her job and colleagues, and owed Sullivan Foods for where she was today.

That rationale was Olivia's grievous mistake. It was abundantly clear from Catherine's email that Olivia was an employee of Sullivan Foods and nothing more.

The most painful betrayal is always from the people you trust the most.

Broken and exhausted, Olivia curled up on the couch with Oreo and cried.

Part I

The Beginning

Life is inherently unfair and pride is a commodity.

—M.L. Lexi

Chapter 1

UNEMPLOYMENT IS A mixed bag. The downside is uncertainty, and the upside is the freedom to do what you enjoy on your terms.

Five months on, Olivia was an unemployed middle age, menopausal woman with a deflated ego. Her wardrobe now consisted of shapeless gray sweatpants, a matching sweatshirt, and running shoes. She wore no makeup, and her idea of hair styling was to drag wet fingers through her hair and bundle it into a ponytail.

At fifty-four, Olivia was in the prime of her life with knowledge and experience. Some employers thought so also but weren't willing to pay what she was worth. Many, however, thought otherwise, and the rejections were piling up.

Life didn't seem to hold a lot of promise.

With nowhere to go and too much time on her hands, what Olivia opted to do to process the lingering resentment, anger, and bitterness from her forced departure from Sullivan's was to write. Olivia had always wanted to write. Now, she planned to write the tell-all book to expose the skeletons in the closets of everyone at Sullivan's, who'd made her life a miserable hell and were the reason for her demise.

Sitting at the kitchen table in front of her laptop, Olivia inhaled deeply and exhaled slowly. The house was infinitely silent, and the hum of the refrigerator cycling and her breathing were the only sounds in the room. The ceiling light above the oak table shone incandescent on the polished cream-coloured tile. The lingering smell of sautéed garlic and tomato sauce from the pasta dinner Oreo and she had shared hung in the air.

Olivia read what she'd written, and disappointment came quickly. Why she thought she could write a novel was anyone's guess. After months of struggling to write, it became painfully clear she was not the writer she imagined herself to be—another disappointment to add to the many in Olivia's life.

Not only was the writing not moving along as Olivia hoped, but it was proving not to be the therapeutic process she hoped for. Olivia highlighted the three chapters of poorly written diatribe and pressed delete. Good thing pen and paper were outdated. Deleting typed words on the screen was more environmentally friendly than crumpling paper. By Olivia's estimation, she had already gone through several spruce trees in a few weeks.

Olivia tipped back her head and closed her eyes. "Maybe, there's too much of everything in me. Too many emotions are crowding my head to write anything worth reading. That has to be it. Don't you think so?" Olivia looked down at Oreo. Curled at her feet, he looked up at her with big, brown sad eyes. "I knew you'd understand." Olivia picked Oreo up and set him down on her lap.

"Writing out of anger about the people that instigated it isn't conducive to rational thought or good prose." Olivia reached for the glass of wine and knocked Riesling back to wash away the taste of failure. "Thank God for alcohol," she said, tossing back the remaining wine in her glass. The swallow of wine infused Olivia with some vigour. "To hell with Catherine Sullivan, Gabe Greene, and Vince Campbell. To hell with them all."

Setting Oreo down on the floor, Olivia pushed off her desk, stood, and walked toward the French doors. She pushed them open and felt the heat on her face. June had rolled in hot and dry. The air smelled of earth, mowed grass, and the sweet scents from the garden.

"Go on, Oreo, do your thing and don't go chasing after raccoons. You'll lose that fight," she said, and stepped out on the small stone patio.

Soft moonlight spilled from the dark sky, and shadows stretched through the trees and the garden bursting with red roses, pink rhododendrons and bleeding hearts, purple phlox, and a variety of hostas. None of its beauty would exist if Olivia had continued her feeble attempt at gardening and hadn't hired Mr. Green Thumb. Yet another hobby she'd tried in her time off and wrote off along with photography, painting, scrapbooking, knitting, and cross-stitching, all hobbies that turned into a hard no when she realized she hadn't the talent or interest to pursue.

Travelling was on Olivia's bucket list but wasn't a priority. The bustle of airports, crowded planes, and living out of her suitcase wasn't Olivia's idea of pleasure or adventure. Besides, whom would she travel with? Friends had disappeared after she married Bob. He had kept them away during their marriage, and when he left, Olivia was focused on surviving and getting out of debt, not reigniting old friendships.

There was her sister, not that Olivia could pry Lottie from her girls, thirteen-year-old Juliette and twelve-year-old Lexi or her husband, Adam. Being a mom and wife was what Lottie loved, and she wouldn't leave her family to gallivant the world with Olivia.

The writing was all Olivia had and was what she needed to do. Exposing everyone who'd bullied her and made her life a miserable hell to advance their agenda was what she needed to get the anger out of her system. For Olivia, revenge was a dish best served in print for everyone to read. Come hell or high water Olivia would write her book.

Revenge was a dish best served in print for everyone to read.

Chapter 2

THE SCENT OF salt and brine rode on the mist from the vast blue sea. The pulsating sound of waves propelled by a northeast wind rolling ashore and then rearing back for the next pass soothed Olivia. The hot sun poured over her body, glistening under a layer of cocoa butter sunscreen.

Paradise, Olivia thought and wished her butt was planted on the white sand of a Caribbean beach rather than listening to Gabe Greene—the axis of evil—nasal voice scolding her like a child.

Gabe Greene, the head buyer for one of the largest supermarket chains in the country, was every saleswoman's worst nightmare.

From the head of the oval conference table, Olivia watched the dark, beady eyes that sat exceedingly close in a triangular-shaped face above a cut-glass nose. He was a smallish, round man who appeared taller than he was due to the adjustable height on his chair that he cranked up for maximum effect. He wore a blue cashmere sweater over a soft blue shirt and black slacks. His clothes were worth more than ten of the navy-blue tapered pants suit Olivia wore and did nothing for him. An asshole in fine clothes was still an asshole.

What Gabe Greene lacked in personality, he made up in volume. For the past thirty minutes, the volume was dialled up to the maximum as Gabe beat his flabby chest to assert his male supremacy over Olivia.

Condescending asshole, Olivia thought, but she was a professional or that's what she told herself to maintain her composure. No matter how often she'd endured Gabe's verbal abuse in the past fifteen years, it never got easier.

"You don't do anything without my approval, and you sure as hell don't ship your crap to my stores without it," Gabe said with an imperial tone.

"You mean daddy's stores," Olivia murmured to herself.

Olivia wore a white shirt beneath the single-button jacket and pants accentuating curves rounded over the years. Age, lack of exercise, and genetics tend to do that to a body, although Olivia carried the extra weight proportionately well. She wore flat patent shoes. Comfort over sexuality, the last thing Olivia wanted was to bring sexuality to a meeting with Gabe Greene.

"You answer to me."

Olivia imagined it took all his strength to bite back the "you fucking bitch" segue he wanted to say.

"Me, and only me, has the last word. I don't answer to you or your company." He held his hand up, palm out, to silence Olivia when she opened her mouth to remind him he had authorized the purchase and shipment. "If I want your input, I'll ask for it." His angry stance made him seem like the asshole he was, but he seemed pleased with it.

Gabe rolled into his next rant with the breath of dragons, and the muscles in Olivia's stomach clamped into the tight knots of nerves he always brought on. She could do with some Johnny Walker courage right then. Johnny Walker not available, as an alternative, Olivia lowered her hands to her lap and snapped the elastic band on her wrist to control her anxiety.

Studying the dark eyes lit with anger, Olivia wondered if Gabe knew how much a douche he was. Did his douchery come naturally?

"I," Gabe stabbed a stiff sausage-thick finger into his flabby chest, "have the ultimate word. Not you or that insignificant, misguided company that insists on keeping such an incompetent as you on their payroll." Sweat pearled on his bald, bowling-ball-shaped head.

Olivia determined that pent-up sexual frustration made Gabe such an asshat because who'd sleep with a toad. As sex-starved as she was, even a million-dollar offer to spend five minutes with him wouldn't tempt Olivia into the heinous deed.

Gabe went on with the tirade. If I were your boss, I'd have gotten rid of you long ago," he spat with authority.

Olivia snapped the elastic band faster. Her wrist was turning a deep apple-red.

Gabe was one of her largest customers, making her the commission that kept a roof over her head and food on the table, and he knew it. Olivia's patience, however, was wearing thin. The funny thing about patience was that it frayed with age. At fifty-four, Olivia's was paper-thin. She was too old to put up with the unwarranted rants of a man compensating for the tiny penis between the short, stubby legs.

Gabe rose and slammed his palms on the table with the force his five-two frame allowed. And another thing...."

In a fleeting lapse of control, at the opposite end of the table, Olivia rose to her five-four height, plunked her hands on the table, and aimed lit blue eyes at Gabe. Shut the fuck up, you insignificant little man. I've put up with your bullshit for too long and got an ulcer in the process.

If only your mouth and ego were as small as your," her eyes lowered below his waist, "fragile manhood."

Seeing the cocky look on Gabe's face wane into a dazed, stunned stare gave Olivia the strength to go on.

"Does debasing people, women, in particular, make you feel like the man you're not?" When you're in the hole, stop digging, said the sensible Olivia in her head, but she'd endured the annoying toad and swallowed her pride for too long to stop. She plowed on. "You're lucky daddy owns the company and has given you the unearned title, the unearned respect, and that huge entitlement you carry with arrogance. No other company would allow a sexist, uncouth pig like you to do so."

The expression on Gabe's face was that of a cornered four-year-old, and by Christ, it felt great. Olivia's nerves relaxed, and the pressure in her chest subsided.

Olivia's confidence was soaring like a vulture hovering over death, and she went on. "Any other company would have cut ties with a close-minded, dimwitted employee like you long ago. I have many more adjectives, and none of them pleasant, but you're not worth my time and energy."

Shock glazed Gabe's eyes; all he did was stare at Olivia.

"What's wrong little man? Oh, did I hurt your feelings, Gabi?"

"Don't call me that."

"Oops, touched on some mommy or daddy issues, did I, Gabi?" Olivia watched the flush rise to her cheeks. Nothing had ever felt better. Someone rebuking you doesn't sit so well with you. Imagine how your self-important twaddle has made countless women, including me, who've put up with your bullshit for the years just to put food on the table feel. I'll tell you something, Gabi."

Olivia held up a finger to silence Gabe when he opened his mouth.

"Oh no, no, no, you're not interrupting me. Telling you how much of a giant asswipe you are feels great. I should have told you off a long time and saved me tons of money on Tums." Olivia gathered her papers off the table and tossed them into her briefcase. This is my first time leaving you without my stomach in knots."

"You know you can kiss your account and commissions goodbye," Gabe said when he found his voice.

The heat in Olivia's eyes evaporated, and a smile now filled them. "Hear that? It's the sound of me not giving a flying rat's ass. And you will continue to buy from us."

He set his teeth against his temper. "I don't think so."

"Oh, but you will."

Gabe slammed a hand on the table. "Get the fuck out of her."

Olivia sank back in her chair. "How do you suppose daddy will react when I wrongly text him confirming your monthly kickback envelope has been dropped off?"

"That's a serious accusation and completely untrue." Gabe's hands went into tight fists.

"Tap, tap, tap." Olivia mimicked typing on her cell phone. "Hello Gabe, kickback envelope dropped off as requested at your home in the special mailbox at the side of the house. It's the yellow envelope amongst all the envelopes from your other suppliers." She tapped the send button on her cell phone. "You didn't think I knew of your agreement with Vince made behind my back?" Olivia finished.

Savouring the sweet taste of success and feeling empowered, with her head held high, Olivia walked out of the conference room to face a waiting room of salespeople's eyes aimed at her in admiration.

"Epic, Oliva," Tracy commented with a wink.

Aurora gave Olivia the subtle chin tilt of gratitude.

"The cojones on you, Olivia, are boulder size," said Martin.

That's how Olivia wished the meeting had gone, but in the reality that was her life, she'd sat through Gabe's rebuking in silence. Biting her tongue, Olivia apologized to him because, unlike Gabe, she couldn't bank on nepotism to survive the verbal attack rolling in her head.

Olivia Falco was a woman whose husband cleaned out their bank account and walked out on her after their ten-year marriage. With seven months of back mortgage and a stack of unpaid bills, she accepted the first and only job to come her way.

Olivia Falco was a woman who was grateful to Sullivan Foods for giving her the job when no one else would. She gave everything she had to the company working her way from receptionist to the Director of Sales.

A middle-aged, menopausal, childless, single woman, Olivia Falco, was damned if she would jeopardize everything she worked hard for because of an insecure man with daddy issues. If putting up with an asshole like Gabe was what she had to do, it's what she'd do.

That was who Olivia Falco was.

What Olivia needed at that moment was a sugary treat. A few more pounds to the thirty she'd put on in the past few years wasn't going to make a difference.

OLIVIA READ WHAT SHE WROTE AND liked it. "This is good, Oreo." Oreo barked his tacit agreement. "Yeah, I know. I'll change the names on the edit. This is only a draft. I just had to get into the moment. Pouring myself, not just my anger, into my story was what I was missing. You, my beautiful boy, are a great inspiration."

Now there was another louder bark.

"In the words of C.S. Lewis, onward and upward, Oreo." Olivia set up the next chapter.

Chapter 3

AFTER HER MEETING with Gabe, Olivia headed to the nearby coffee shop to buy the donuts and coffee she didn't need or want. Stress eating was an essential component of a Gabe meeting.

The streets were plowed clean of the snow that fell overnight, and a late morning sun falling over the city melted the remaining patches.

At the Coffee's Up drive-through, Olivia picked up the sugary treat and caffeine necessary to ease the anxiety Gabe's meeting caused before heading back to the office. The late morning traffic on highway 401 was bumper-to-bumper, moving at snail speed. Olivia downed the cinnamon cruller, honey glaze donut, and coffee with one hand on the steering wheel drumming to Toto's Africa flowing from the car radio.

There was nothing like a sugar high to lift the spirits.

Forty minutes later, Olivia steered the car into Sullivan Foods' parking lot. Her sugar high flatlined, and the anxiety was back, stabbing at the center of her chest. Feeling like she'd traded one hell for another, Olivia parked the car and left the engine running with the heat cranked up against the January cold. The Boomtown Rats came on the car radio, affirming how much they hated Mondays. She sat there for a while, staring at the front door dreading going in.

It hadn't been that way when she started working at Sullivan, but then need, naiveté, gullibility, and youthful energy blinded you to the realities of life. The eyes of a twenty-nine-year-old saw things differently than those of a fifty-four-year-old.

There was a time Olivia looked forward to getting up in the morning and going to work. The sense of accomplishment for a job well done was absolute. The camaraderie that once existed among the staff gave Olivia a sense of belonging and a feeling of mine-ness.

If only there were a do-over for people who've lived years of their life and gathered valuable intel. People didn't have a delete button to erase past mistakes. If she had the capability, Olivia would erase the one mistake that altered her life's course and put her on the downhill trajectory she had to scale for what felt like an eternity.

If she'd taken the correct path on the forked road at nineteen, Olivia's life would be very different now. She would have pursued the journalism degree she dreamed of and not married young. And she wouldn't have married Bob and ended up here. But that chapter of Olivia's life was inked, and there were no rewrites.

Olivia swept disappointment aside. Psyching herself to face another day, she exited the car and walked through Sullivan's front door.

Brewing coffee from the lunchroom scented the air. Sunlight pouring from the entrance-facing glass walls lit the office bright. The carpet was a gray, thick pile, and the walls were steel blue with colourful abstract artwork. Over the murmur of conversation, cell phones shrilled, and keyboards clattered under tapping fingers. Printers and photocopiers whirred as they rolled out printed paper.

There were few offices, with a large, open space in the centre with desks lined in four rows. Catherine believed in the open concept office mainly because it gave her an unobtrusive view of the staff's comings and goings.

Behind the reception desk Sondra Coleman, receptionist extraordinaire and Olivia's only ally in the company of fifty employees, staffed the cell phone.

Long mink-coloured curls spilled around a heart-shaped face. Round, raven-black eyes were dusted bronze, and the full lips painted red. The lemon-yellow blouse Sondra wore over an exceptionally short pleated skirt set off the flawless, silk-black skin Olivia envied.

Olivia set her briefcase and car keys on the desk's edge. "Hey…." She stopped when Sondra pointed a finger with an exceedingly long, polished nail that matched her lipstick to the headset nested in her hair to indicate she was on a call. "Sorry," Olivia murmured and shrugged out of her coat.

"You didn't get my message," Sondra said, pressing the release button on the switchboard cell phone.

"No, I had to get into my car and as far away as quickly as possible from Gabe Greene."

"Giant douche was as douchy as ever?"

"The man cannot not be an asshole. As we walked out of the conference room, he got a call, and I saw the caller's name on his phone screen. The Bitch, turned out to be his soon-to-be ex-wife."

"She didn't dodge that bullet soon enough." Sondra reached into her tote for the tube of lipstick and compact mirror. "You better be putting all this into your book. That boy needs a good ego whipping."

"Oh, it's going in." Olivia ran her fingers over her front teeth. "Lipstick. So, what was the message?"

"Catherine's been asking for you." Sondra wiped her teeth with a tissue and flashed them at Olivia.

"Lipstick's gone. What does Catherine want?"

"You forgot again. And here's me thinking you intentionally scheduled the meeting with Gabe this morning to skip Catherine's team-building meeting."

"Shit, I did forget. This day keeps on getting better." Olivia stared at the reflection on the mirrored wall behind Sondra displaying Sullivan Foods in black letters and studied the woman she saw.

Shoulder-length chestnut hair—L'Oréal had a hand in that—sea-blue eyes and full lips. Her wrinkle-free face, due to great genetics passed on by her mother, made her look ten years younger.

Her sister wasn't so lucky. Ten years her junior, Lottie's genetic makeup was mainly paternal. Lottie, the perfect mother of two and wife to Adam, was flawless in every way, except for the roadmap of her life etched on her face.

"When you didn't return my call, Catherine held the meeting off for as long as she could, not that I would have told her if you had called. Still, she only started the meeting half an hour ago."

"Shit, so…"

"Yep, it's going to go on for another hour or two. You know how much Catherine loves a captive audience and the sound of her voice. She told me to send you in the moment you arrived. My message warned you to stay away until after lunch."

"What stage are they at?"

"I heard something about silos. Apparently, each one of us is a silo. She spewed some bullshit about how the disproportionate heights of the silos affect office morale.

She then closed the door to prying ears. As if I could give a flying rat's ass about anything she said. The woman is batshit crazy." The cell phone rang, and Sondra eyed it with disdain.

"Go ahead, get it."

"It'll go to voicemail. I wish people would stop calling," Sondra said when two more lines lit up on the phone.

"You're a receptionist." Olivia pointed out.

"And your point is."

Olivia rolled her eyes to the heavens. "Sorry, I lost my mind for a moment."

"You have time to sneak out before Mrs. Batshit Crazy sees you."

"Olivia, there you are." Catherine Sullivan, tall, slim, elegant, and as blonde as a bottle of peroxide could make the pin-straight hair, stepped out of the meeting room and closed the door behind her.

Catherine was in her seventies—her actual age was a guarded secret. Her clothes bespoke designer labels and money. Today, she'd paired high black boots with pointed heels, a Chanel skirt and double-breasted jacket pants in ivory. She wore diamonds on her ears, long neck, and thin wrists. Her blond hair was slicked back with enough product to be a fire hazard.

"I've been holding off the best part of the meeting for you. We're about to review the assigned reading material," Catherine said.

"Sure. Yeah. Sorry. I had a meeting with Gabe Greene this morning."

"Wait backward, record scratch. You give your grown-ass executive team reading homework?" Sondra said without masking her shock.

"Reading The Art Of The Compromise is not just homework, Sondra. It's a concept I want my squabbling executives to embrace. Internal strife is not what Sullivan Foods is about."

"Pfft, it has been since I can remember," Sondra said, and Olivia cleared her throat to disguise a laugh.

"You'd do well to read it, Sondra. I have extra copies of the book in my office," Catherine said.

"I'm good. Mama always says, 'My Sandi, that's what Mama calls me, is nothing if not the embodiment of compromise.'" The innocent gleam in Sondra's eyes had Olivia biting back a snort of laughter.

"Yes, Sondra, you certainly are." The sarcasm spewed from Catherine's pink-lipsticked mouth.

"Thank you for recognizing it, Catherine." Sondra bit into the brownie square she dug from the Tupperware in her top desk drawer. "Brownie?"

"No, thank you," Catherine said to Olivia's great relief.

"You sure? I know they're fattening, but they're chocolatey and great for the soul." Sondra's testicular fortitude was enviable. To offer pot-laced brownies to their tight-ass septuagenarian boss was something only Sondra could do.

"She's sure, Sondra." Olivia's blue eyes cut away from Sondra to Catherine. "I'll be right in, Catherine. I need a minute to drop my things at my desk." With a huff, Olivia tipped back her head when Catherine was out of sight. "I didn't read the goddamn book. I didn't think she was serious about reviewing it. I have better things to do with my time."

"No, you don't." Sondra took a bite of the brownie.

Olivia rolled her eyes slightly upward, looking at Sondra obliquely. "No, I don't. Still, she shouldn't be jamming my time with bullshit reading, and it's not as if that book will help transform us into the love fest she wants."

"After all this time, you should know our dear leader better. Catherine is the queen of ineffectuality."

"Big word."

"Word of the day." Sondra pointed to her desk calendar. "You're way tense, Olive Oyl. Here, you need this more than me." Sondra handed Olivia a piece of the brownie.

"It's laced, isn't it?" Olivia and Malcolm, from IT, the man Sondra lived in the hope of getting into her bed or his, she wasn't fussy, knew of Sondra's baking talent.

"Please, it's me you're talking to," Sondra said, biting into more brownie. "Top class, fair trade weed I got from my brother." She smirked when Olivia's brows lifted. "What? I'm an environmentalist."

"Right. And why offer Catherine a brownie? Do you want to get fired?"

Sondra tossed the remains of her brownie into her mouth and chased it with coffee. "I knew she wouldn't take it. Too many calories, sugar, and sinful pleasure for a tight ass like her."

"What if she had taken it?"

Sondra saw Olivia's death glare behind her eyes. "She didn't. Besides, she'd never fire me. Malcolm and I are her token black employees, and Catherine's as white as they come."

"Christ, the things that come out of your mouth."

"You need to chill, babe. Here, take two squares." Sondra flipped the lid on the Tupperware container.

"I can't eat both. I'll be flying as high as a kite through the meeting."

"The only way to go into Catherine's team-building meeting."

Olivia didn't need her arm twisted much.

"I'M ON A ROLL, OREO," OLIVIA shrieked, startling the dog curled at her feet out of his slumber. "And I have to tell you, it feels great." Oreo raised a disapproving eye. "Sorry, I woke you, didn't I? Go back to sleep. I want to get another chapter in before I call it a day." Flexing her fingers, Olivia turned back to the laptop.

Chapter 4

OLIVIA PAUSED WITH her hand on the doorknob. Segueing from a Gabe Greene meeting into Catherine's team-building meeting made the muscles in Olivia's shoulders clench. The pounding headache at the base of her skull felt like her head would explode. She regretted not eating the entire brownie square. Half of a brownie didn't give her the high to help make it through Catherine's crazy fest.

As if Catherine's incompetence wasn't enough, she deluded herself into believing peddling the gibberish, concocted by an unemployed corporate failure with too much time on his hands, to her employees would turn her into the leader she would never be.

Ineptitude blinds people to their failures.

Catherine was as competent as she was a blonde. Her peroxide-soaked brain stopped her from seeing the reality that the company ran smoother when without her.

Catherine's tactics were dated. Berating and embarrassing the staff around the conference table during a meeting may have been considered motivation in her days, but it wasn't now. By Catherine's reasoning, embarrassing employees and turning them against each other bred competition and the incentive to succeed.

Uninvolved in the daily operation of the company she built decades ago, Catherine knew little of its operation and cared less about keeping up with the modern-day processes that made her business profitable and efficient. Her lackadaisical attitude and ignorance made her decision-making capabilities nonexistent. Catherine was a relic of the past with nothing constructive or of interest to say. Still, she could outtalk a parrot on meth, and meetings were her outlet for her boundless gum-flapping energy.

Catherine held nonsensical meetings to discuss futile matters. There were breakfast meetings to discuss whatever came to mind in sleep, during lunch, or on her drive home. There were late afternoon follow-ups to Brainstorm the early morning meeting.

When Catherine learned the workings of the company's online calendar, accessible by all the employees, Malcolm went into hiding when threatened with a beating by the staff. Moving forward, Catherine logged meetings into the calendar. Now, no one could claim amnesia.

But where there's a will, there's a way. Overnight, the staff became inundated with work and unable to attend Catherine's meetings.

Bracing for the blow, Olivia opened the door to the conference room. All eyes pivoted to her, and she felt like the portly eight-year-old walking into the second-grade classroom. It felt like all kinds of wrong then, and it felt like all kinds of wrong now.

"Ah, Olivia, take a seat. No, my love, don't sit so far from us. Wheel your chair closer to the table," Catherine said when Olivia sat at the chair, pushed against the back wall farthest from the table to fade into the background. Reluctantly, Olivia moved close to the table. "We were discussing…." Catherine went on, and the pain inside Olivia's skull thumped harder.

Olivia's gaze moved around the room, scanning the faces around the polished mahogany table. All her archenemies were in attendance.

Vince Campbell, V.P. of Sales. Every company had one person who took delight in the view from their boss's colon, and Vince Campbell was Sullivan's. He would throw his back out to get the ideal view from Catherine's butt.

Across him, Elvira White, Vince's Director of National Sale and bed warmer, fluttered long mascaraed lashes above blue eyes at him. Elvira was medium height and the live version of a Barbie doll. She had long blonde hair, pouty lips, and the athletic, curvy body that today featured a low-cut, tight-fitting sweater and pants that turned heads young and old, male and female, when she walked into a room.

Next to her was Molly Garcia, the VP of Purchasing. Molly came with the education that met Catherine's stringent requirements. Although, how a bachelor in Fine Arts correlated to food buying was a feat Molly had yet to scale. The same went for Trish, the VP of Accounting, who was scared of her own shadow.

Optimism was the eternal spring of hope at Sullivan Foods.

The room filled with VPs—Sullivan's hierarchy was inordinately top-heavy—Catherine babbled on. She tossed the latest corporate buzzword, synergy, incentivize, game-changer, and overarching, into her sermon. As if the words would magically turn Sullivan's into a love-fest. As if it was going to make Vince Campbell less detestable, Elvira less duplicitous, or sprinkle magical competent dust on everyone.

"I want my children," Catherine spread arms wide, "to work together, get along, and respect one another."

Olivia thought this was coming from the woman who hitched her wagon to Vince, a backstabbing antagonizer who did what was necessary to achieve his goal of world domination.

"Trish, tell us which character in the book you relate to and why?" Catherine said to the introverted number cruncher. The flush rose to Trish's cheeks, and she stumbled through her response.

Olivia's eyes circling the table, she heard Catherine's crazy—egged on by Vince—progress into the absurd. "To summarize, for Olivia's sake. We're working in silos, and each of our silos is at varying levels creating an imbalance. Trish's is half-full and Molly's three-quarters empty, whereas Vince's and Elvira's are full of positive energy." Catherine gave Vince a little smirk that made Olivia wince. "Olivia, yours is nearly empty, devoid of positive energy, and we must get that rectified. Yes, Olivia." Olivia would stab her eyes if she could. "I want everyone to aim for their silos to be as full as Vince's."

The crazy was dialled high today, Olivia thought, nodding her head.

Catherine wasn't done. "Only when everyone's silos are levelled can we come together and make this company work. Symmetry, children, think symmetry. Understand, Olivia?"

Olivia made a sound of assent because not agreeing was futile. Catherine didn't live in reality and couldn't see the truth. People were too self-serving and ready to plunge the knife at anyone's back who obstructed their way up the corporate ladder to allow a united front. And Vince was a climber of ladders, and she was his enabler.

Vince was Catherine's voice of authority, her Tom Hagen, her maharishi, but his vision wasn't in Sullivan's or Catherine's interest. Vince wanted to take Sullivan Foods from Catherine, but blinded by his charm, she failed to see what was happening under her nose.

"Thank you for sharing, Trish. Vince, share your thoughts," Catherine said.

Vince dutifully complied. "Thank you for asking, Catherine." His swatch of dark hair matched the colour of the wide-set eyes. He had a pointy nose set in a sloped face with a scruff of a goatee. His skin was pasty-white, and he had as many redeeming qualities as the fit of the gray sweater over a blue shirt and black pants on his flabby body. "I'm grateful for your foresight and bringing this team-building exercise to the staff to unite us. It's the sign of true leadership." Vince shot Catherine a smile that sent her tumbling into love.

Olivia swallowed a bit of regurgitated brownie. If Vince tried harder to dole out that bogus charm, he might set himself on fire. Olivia hoped he would.

"In this insightful read you brought to our attention, Catherine, I see myself as…." Vince droned on like someone selling useless crap on a late-night infomercial.

The interminable infomercial of himself droned on for an eternity. Everyone's eyes were focused on Vince, but no one but Catherine and Elvira listened to his dribble.

What Elvira saw in the man was a mystery to Olivia. Her shortcomings were many. For starters, she had the IQ of a sloth and a viperous personality, but she was a knockout able to have any man she wanted.

"Synergy, as Catherine said, is our goal," Vince said.

Olivia thought the man couldn't spell the word and absently chortled a snort.

"Olivia, if you have something to add, please share." Vince leaned forward in his chair, and his floppy ears seemed to flop with the move.

Regretting not eating both brownie squares, Olivia tugged on the rubber band at her wrist.

"We'd all like to hear from you," Vince said without any intonation of interest. The man fed on the power of making others feel small. It was as necessary to his inflated ego as the air he breathed.

The muscle in Olivia's jaw began to twitch, and she tugged on the rubber band at her wrist to calm herself.

"We're waiting, Olivia. Please, tell us your thoughts," Vince proded.

Olivia's eyes went hard, and her hands tightened into fists. Vice might be the man Catherine turned to when she couldn't make a decision. He might be Catherine's voice of authority, but to everyone else, he was a bombastic, arrogant buffoon.

Olivia replayed the dialogue she'd played thousands of times in her head. Summoning the courage, she sat spear-straight in her chair and flashed lit blue eyes at Vince. "You're a deceitful fraud who's taking advantage of an attention-seeking, old woman to take over her company. Your so-called winning personality hazes Catherine's vision but no one else's. We all see through you." Nerves bouncing, Olivia stalked the room with pep and vigour, and every eye followed her.

"My Bullshit Perception Scale works just fine, Vince, and you tip that scale to the max. You have no interest in bettering the company or taking care of the employee's needs. Your sole interest is in stroking your ego." Olivia shook her head and levelled her eyes at Catherine. "Open your eyes, for God's sake. He's trying to steal the company from under you?" Olivia fell back in her chair. "Christ! My feet have ached from treading on so many eggshells since you hired this fucking bottom feeder."

Catherine's brown eyes and those around the table widened, while Vince's face and the tips of his ears turned deep red.

The satisfaction Olivia felt at exposing Vince was immeasurable. Undoubtedly, Catherine and the staff would be grateful for opening their eyes. Uncertainty had them walking in a daze since Vince appeared three years ago. No one felt secure at their job, and morale was at its lowest.

The truth was out, and they would finally get answers.

"I've only said what everyone, but you, Catherine, is thinking and saying behind your back."

"Olivia. Olivia," Catherine called out when Olivia remained silent. "As Vince said, we're interested to hear what you have to say."

Olivia swallowed hard.

Vince could see Olivia's obvious discomfort, and his lips curled into a smug grin. Olivia imagined knocking out his overly bleached teeth.

"Don't be shy, Olivia. Everyone's input is essential to our success," said Vince.

Fading into the background is an underrated art form, Olivia thought as she coughed into her hand to compose herself and the response Catherine and Vince wanted to hear.

THE GLOW OF DELIGHT ON OLIVIA'S face, she saved her work and shut down the laptop for the night. Oreo lay still at her feet. Curled tightly, his head on his front paws, his snore sounded like a foghorn at sea. Olivia bent down and ran a hand over his head. Her soothing touch woke him, and he raised a groggy eye to her.

"Go on up to the bedroom. I'll be there shortly." Olivia watched Oreo amble out the kitchen and up the stairs. "Not on my bed, Oreo, but yours."

Oreo stopped, turned his head slightly and gave her a slanted look before going on his way.

"Well, I've been told." Olivia picked up her wine glass and walked to the open French doors.

The air was redolent with the rich scents of lilac and roses. Above, stars as clear as glass against a black sky shimmered under the glow of a sliced moon.

The night was meant for lovers, but Olivia wouldn't know about that. It had been so long since she'd had a man in her life or bed. Oreo was the closest she came to male companionship and just as well since Bob quelled the need for men.

Olivia was fine on her own. She had Oreo, a loyal companion who loved her and did what he was told. Olivia had underway the first draft of her revenge book, and her writing juices kindled. Her life would be perfect if only she could eliminate the gnawing feeling in her stomach.

Chapter 5

NOT ALL DAYS were terrible, and not all customers were Gabe.

John Kennedy was Olivia's favourite and largest buyer and Gabe's antithesis. John was the type of person who compensated for the Gabes of the world. He made you believe the world wasn't all fire and brimstone and filled your wretched existence with a warm pleasure.

John was a large man, vertically and in circumference, who sat in a small cubicle with gray walls and no door. The size of the cubicle didn't bother John as much as the lack of a door did.

The doorless cubicle didn't sit well with him, and he was vocal about it because it was a demonstrable gesture from those above him. The respect he got from his chain of command for the millions of dollars in revenue he generated for the company was minimal.

The cubicle was six by six square feet and part of the rat maze to accommodate two-hundred employees on the fourth floor. A tan three-door cabinet stood against one wall. A bulletin board with a tacked-on calendar, assortment of notes, and competitor's flyers hung on the wall facing John's desk. The desk was inordinately organized—for a man—with only the necessities to execute the daily grind. There was a laptop, stapler and a stapler remover, two pencils and two pens stacked in a #1 Dad cup, and the IN and OUT trays overflowed with paperwork. The floor was carpeted gray, and the white lights above were bright.

Reaching for the jar of cashews, John unscrewed the lid and tipped it toward Olivia. She opened her hand, palm up. "Sample from the Nutty Nuts people. I don't know what they put in this stuff, but Jesus on a bicycle, it's mmm," he hummed and tossed a few nuts into his mouth.

John wore neatly pressed jeans with a sky blue shirt and running tan loafers. John said he was married with two kids and fussing over his appearance wasn't a priority.

Olivia tossed the three nuts in her pal m into her mouth. "That is good." In a tan V-neck sweater and moss-green pants, Olivia equaled John's underdressed appearance. When in Rome.

John tipped a few more cashews into Olivia's hand and took a few for himself. "So, I have good news for you."

She looked at John. He was wearing a gray polo shirt with the company logo, *The Market*, embroidered on the left hand pocket over faded blue jeans. "You do."

John started to speak but stopped when his assistant, Tasha, poked her head in the open doorway. "Hey, Olivia."

"Hey, Tasha. How are you doing?"

"Living the dream." Tasha leaned on the cubicle wall with her arms folded. Her charcoal black hair matched her eyes, and her lips were glossy red. She was twenty-five years old and in a perpetual state of happiness. Olivia envied her. "Cake is happening for Dicky in the boardroom. There are four mouthwatering cakes, black forest, carrot, cheesecake, and red velvet to choose from."

"Dicky is loved," said Olivia.

John smiled. "Dicky is loved, but the cakes are samples, and if I know Tasha, she'll sample all of them. She becomes unbearable if she doesn't get her mid-morning cake fix."

Natasha leaned her shoulder into the doorframe. "He knows me well. Can you also read what I'm thinking?"

"I'd report you to HR if I could bring myself to repeat the sordid words," John answered with humour in his eyes.

"He does read minds." There was a trace of humour at the corners of Tasha's mouth.

John laughed and exclaimed, "Yours only."

"I'll bring you a piece of your fave, black forest. Would you like a piece, Olivia?" Tasha offered.

Olivia looked at tall, thin Natasha. "Unlike you, I don't burn calories by merely breathing."

The off-key chant of happy birthday rang out, followed by clapping. "I better get in line for our piece, or we may end up cakeless. See you, Olivia."

"See you, Tasha," Olivia said as friendly chatter broke out from the conference room when the birthday boy cut into his cake. Olivia envied the camaraderie. It was so long since she'd heard laughter at Sullivan's or felt as harmonious.

"Back to business." John sank his corpulent frame back in his swivel chair. "You won the bid for the summer program, but I think it'll become a permanent item on our store shelves."

Olivia stared for a moment. "Really?"

John leaned in to type on his laptop. "I'm emailing you the delivery schedule and our terms, standard gobbledygook. We forecast sales of five million dollars the first year and triple by the fourth."

Olivia smiled inwardly until John said, "By the way, who's Vince Campbell?"

Olivia felt the center of her stomach begin to pinch and wind tight. "He's our VP of Sales. Why do you ask?"

"He's left several messages asking for a meeting with me." The words felt like a solid punch to Olivia's gut, one she should have been prepared for. She should have known Vince would circumvent her and attempt to steal her customers from under her. "I don't know why he wants to meet, but will you let him know I'm dealing with you, and I only want to deal with you." John pressed send on the email.

"Yes, of course. My apologies, John. I'm sure it's an oversight on his part." Though Olivia's voice was calm, fire rode in her eyes.

A GLASS OF ZINFANDEL IN HAND, Olivia leaned back on the couch and looked beyond the window with a view of the front yard and street. It was close to midnight, nothing stirred, and cones of light from the lampposts lighted the street.

"Fifth chapter completed," she said to Oreo spread out next to her, his head resting on his front paws. "There's a lot of revision and editing to follow. That's a given, and I'm good with that." Olivia's problem was she wasn't getting that innate feeling of sureness about her book, its content, or the story's framework. Olivia mulled that for a moment.

She had no fully developed plan for her book. Olivia wrote as the words and thoughts came to get her writing juices flowing. A matter of degree and method, but she had limited savings to let inspiration drift for too long. She needed to get her book—The Pissed Woman was the tentative working title—written, published, and making money in twelve months. A bold unrealistic plan, Olivia knew that. Few authors made money, let alone generated an income from their books in a matter of months.

That's all Olivia had and what she would hang onto.

Five chapters in five months were something she supposed. "I never thought I'd get this far in, good or bad writing as it may be, feels great, Oreo," she said, and Oreo looked at her without any expression before he turned belly up for rubs, and Olivia obliged as he knew she would.

With the taste of sweet wine on her tongue, Olivia took pleasure from her meagre accomplishment because it was the first time she felt good about herself and life in a long while.

Life did seem to hold a lot of promise, Olivia thought philosophically.

Chapter 6

EARLY MORNING SUN washing out of a cloudless summer sky cut through the cut-glass window of the French doors and spilled light into Olivia's kitchen.

The kitchen was a small but functional space due to Lottie's insistence that Olivia modernizes the forty-year-old room. Lottie fought Olivia tooth and nail to let her modernize, and when she did, the result was a stunning contemporary look.

Shiny, ivory tiles replaced the decades-old faded linoleum. Walls painted to match the tiles made the kitchen appear bigger and airy. Pressed-board cupboards came down, and blonde oak wood and a white quartz countertop went up. Although perfectly functioning after four decades, Lottie swapped the canary-yellow Westinghouse refrigerator and stove with modern stainless steel appliances.

"I thought that would get you out of bed and downstairs." This morning, Olivia traded from the typical gray sweatpants and sweatshirt to a bright pale purple. Her hair was caught back, tied with a black scrunchie. "Breakfast will be served in ten minutes." Oreo propped himself on his rump next to his bowl and lapped his muzzle.

Early morning sun washing out of a cloudless summer sky cut through the cut-glass window of the French doors and spilled light into the room.

Multi-tasking, Olivia ran a spoon through the eggs to scramble them while she poured coffee into the white cup she picked up from the dish rack. Olivia chopped three slices of bacon and sprinkled it on Oreo's dog food. Plating eggs, bacon, and slices of toast for herself, Olivia walked to the dark oak table at the centre of the room.

"If I continue to eat this way, I'll need to start an exercise regimen, cardio, running, biking, something," she said to Oreo, watching him lick his bowl clean. Bacon had that effect on everyone. "If only I enjoyed exercise." Olivia scooped the last scrambled egg on her plate with buttered toast and chased it with the last of her coffee.

The dishes washed and set to dry on the dishrack Olivia walked to the entry hallway and picked up the lead off the coatrack. "Oreo, walking…." Before she finished, Oreo ran out of the kitchen, raced forward, and slid into Olivia. Olivia raised her eyebrows. "You can really move when you want to."

Oreo gave Olivia a let's-get-on-with-the-walk-woman look.

"You're in for a treat today. After we visit the doggie park, I've decided we're walking an additional fifteen minutes. It's a start to my exercise regimen." Oreo raised one eye, then the other. "Yes, I know it's not much, but fifteen minutes is all the time I can spare. I want to get on the laptop ASAP. I slept well and woke up with many good ideas for my book I want to work on."

STRETCHED OUT ON THE COUCH, WITH the laptop on her lap, Olivia typed.

We form opinions about someone based on what we see on the surface, and what Olivia saw in Vince was the entitled, deceitful, scheming, and lying sonofabitch he was.

For all his Neanderthal pulsating maleness, Vince wasn't very bright.

Not exactly, a well-planned takeover Vince choreographed by calling John Kennedy, a customer Olivia helped make his career, behind her back. Then, men like Vince assumed every man was a disloyal, power-hungry, sexist pig.

Olivia knew Vince's attacks were a projection of his insecurity, but that didn't make it easier to deal with his duplicity.

A sugar treat was necessary to quell the fury brewing in her.

Pulling the car out of John Kennedy's office parking lot, Olivia aimed her eyes out the windshield of her car. Below the staggeringly blue sky that domed the city, Olivia spotted the Starbucks sign. She made a quick right turn into the parking lot past the lights and pulled the car into the first available spot.

The chatter of stylish yuppie coffee drinkers and the strong smell of coffee filled the room. With jazzy sounds floating from the speakers over the heads of the customers, Olivia settled into the empty table by the window to enjoy the coffee and blueberry muffin with a side order of buttered bagel.

Savouring the buttered bagel, Olivia considered taking up exercising as she bit into her bagel. Thirty pounds and climbing had her considering running, cardio, possibly swimming. The possibilities were endless, but Olivia didn't take long to dismiss them all. Dwelling on a pipe dream was futile. Olivia didn't enjoy exerting herself, her body didn't appreciate it, and the outcome of exercise was often injury.

The high caloric, carbohydrate delight enjoyed, Olivia got in her car and reluctantly headed to the office.

The car radio blasting loud, Olivia rocked with Bon Jovi's It's My Life and didn't let herself think about Vince once.

Her drive was a rocking one until she pulled into Sullivan's parking lot. Her shoulders tense and stomach muscles tightening, Oliva parked by the side entrance she'd been relegated to when Vince came aboard. Olivia didn't care about trivialities such as parking. The implication of being pushed out by the gesture concerned her.

Squaring her shoulders, Olivia walked around the building and pushed the front door open.

From behind the receptionist's desk, Sondra looked up. "Hey, babe, how do?" Her hair, smoothed back tight, was wound into a bun, and her pretty face was expertly made up.

"Hey, got you a bagel and cream cheese." Olivia set the bag on the desk.

"Ah, thanks, Olive Oyl. You're a superstar." Sondra's slash of dark eyebrow rose. "You're bursting with news, aren't you?"

Olivia flashed a grin. "I am. Is Catherine in?"

"She's having one of her love-fests in the conference room. She forced the entire office to attend this one."

"You're not there."

"I'm essential staff and must remain to man the switchboard." The cell phone rang, and Sondra let it go to voicemail.

"That's what you told her to bail."

"You know me so well." Sondra slathered cream cheese onto the bagel.

"What's this love-fest for?"

"Vince closed on a one million dollar deal, and she's gathered everyone into the circle of love to bow to the overlord and sing The Circle Of Life while she holds him up by his tiny dick and swirls in slow motion."

Olivia made a little snorting laugh. "Christ! You do have a way with words. Maybe you should be writing my dream book and not me."

"Nah, too much effort, and I'm a firm believer in an effortless life. So, what's your news? Did you finally get laid?" Sondra bit into the bagel, leaving traces of cream cheese around her mouth.

"Is that all you think about?"

"What else is there?" Sondra wiped her mouth with the paper napkin she had dug out from the bag.

"Oh, I don't know, cooking, baking, gardening, painting…."

Sondra lifted her brows. "Aren't those all the things you hate?"

Olivia sighed. "Yeah, they are."

"So, what's your news?" The cell phone rang, and Sondra reached for her coffee cup. Her callous indifference was enviable.

"I closed on a five-million-dollar deal, with the potential to turn into fifteen."

Sondra flashed an all-perfect-teeth smile. "Congrats, Olive Oyl. Go downstairs and announce it to the team. That news will make Vince's tiny brain shrivel even more, not that it can get any smaller than it already is."

Olivia shook her head. "Not my style. Besides, nothing can trump Vince's news. I'll be at my desk."

THE LOVE-FEST WAS A HARD bust. It turned out no one but Catherine and Elvira was interested in stroking Vince's ego or bowing to the wannabe overlord. Twenty minutes into the love-fest, with Vince following close behind, Catherine filed to her office and the staff to their desks.

Two brownies later, balancing on four-inch pointy stilettos, her black leather skirt riding thigh-high, Sondra walked past Olivia's desk on her way to Catherine's office. The glint in Sondra's eyes was intrepid, one of pure mischief fueled partly by THC and partly by her spirit animal, which Olivia thought to be a viper.

Olivia whispered, "Shit, this is not going to be good for anybody."

The staff sensing the same was quiet as they waited for the drama to evolve.

Sondra stood arched in the doorway of Catherine's office to ensure she would remain within everyone's hearing range. "You must be a proud mama of your so accomplished children," Sondra said, watching Elvira pour coffee into two cups and place them before Catherine and Vince at the meeting table. The woman had no pride. "That's some pour skill there, ELVIRA."

Everyone heard the derision in Sondra's voice but stifled the giggle.

"Yes, I am very proud." Catherine flicked worshiping eyes at Vince.

Eww, get a room already. "And so you should be. A six million dollar sale in one day, with a forecasted increase to fifteen, is an achievement to celebrate." From the corner of her eye, Sondra watched Olivia recoil.

Catherine looked at Sondra speculatively before correcting her. "No, dear, it's one million."

"I'm not good at math, but the one million dollar sale from John and the five million from Olivia makes it a total of six." Sondra held six fingers in the air to stress her point. "Add a projected fifteen million dollars in three years, and I call that a sweet day."

Olivia winced. "Oh, Christ."

"From the look of confusion on your face, I gather Olivia hasn't mentioned the deal she closed this morning," Sondra said, and Vince had an instant of pure shock that felt as satisfying to her as a warm pot-laced brownie straight from the oven. "I told Olivia to join the circle of love downstairs and make the announcement, but I guess she didn't. She's very much like you in that respect, Vince. You know, the not blow-your-own-horn type."

Snorted giggles from the staff filled the deafening silence that followed.

"Shit." Olivia shrivelled in her seat.

Vince's mouth clamped hard. His face was expressionless. He drank some more coffee to help swallow the bitter taste of humiliation.

"Anyway, a proud mama, you should be," Sondra added with an impish smile. "Oh, I almost forgot. Vince, you have a message from John Kennedy." Sondra held up the blank note to read. "He says thank you for calling him to request a meeting and is sorry he hasn't returned your many calls, but he already buys our products and is pleased with them and very happy with his salesperson, Olivia." Mama always said: My Sandi is nothing if not diplomatic.

Vince's eyes flashed up at Sondra like two burning flares.

Mentally patting herself in the back, Sondra circled, gave Malcolm a wink, and walked back to her desk.

PUSHING PAST THE EMBARRASSMENT FROM SONDRA's earlier performance, Olivia poked her head into Catherine's office.

"Come in, Olivia." Catherine gestured to the guest chair.

The office was modern and trendy. A round glass table with four chrome and leather overlooked the front garden of the building. Two matching guest chairs faced Catherine's L-shaped desk. Gray vertical blinds shielded the ceiling-to-floor windows.

"I need John Kennedy's contract signed by an officer of the company. I've gone over it, and it's a standard purchaser-vendor agreement. You can have your lawyer review it, but I don't think it necessary." Olivia set the document on Catherine's desk.

Catherine picked up the pages and leafed through them. The cashmere white sweater topped gray straight-leg pants. The outfit came together with black, leather boots. "I'll get Vince to examine it, and he can sign it."

The air hummed between them for thirty seconds as Olivia processed the clear implication Vince had rounded third base and was on his way to heading the company. "If you can get the document signed soon, that would be great." Olivia took a step in retreat toward the door.

"I know you don't like Vince." Catherine sat back in her chair and steepled her fingers under her chin. "Is it because you feel threatened by him?"

Dead silence.

"You don't need to feel threatened by him." Catherine walked to the window and slid the blinds open. "He, like me, is on your side, rooting for you."

Olivia's mind screamed. It would be useless to point out the irony of the statement. Had the woman not heard anything Sondra said?

"I'll be spending less and less time in the office." Catherine sat in her chair. "Vince will be in charge in my absence, and I'd like you to get along with him since you'll be reporting to him."

"Super. Sure. Okay." Olivia smiled a little. "Anything else?"

The sky outside the window suddenly turned dark. In seconds, the snow came hard, hit the window, and made trickle paths down the pane. You could hear the cold wind veering off the lake howl past the window.

"What you did earlier to Vince, through Sondra, was uncalled for."

They looked at each other for a moment.

Olivia set her teeth against the temper brewing in her toward herself for presuming what she did for the company mattered or would be appreciated. Olivia's presumptive stupidity was expected a "well done" or a "congratulations" from Catherine for a job well done. Sullivan's wasn't her company. She was a mere number on a paycheque.

"I want you to apologize to Vince," Catherine said.

Olivia's hands white-knuckled on the back of the guest chair. "I won't apologize to Vince because it's me who should be getting an apology from him for going behind my back to poach my customer. And you, too, owe me an apology for condoning it." Olivia stormed out of the office.

That's not what Olivia said or did. It was what circled in her mind.

Oliva kept a smile in place by visualizing Vince being swallowed into the depths of a burning hell. "Sure. Yeah. Okay. I have to get back to work."

Olivia's contained attitude and body language were overproduced and caused Catherine to say, "I mean it, Olivia."

"Yes, I will apologize," when hell freezes over.

She needed alcohol.

Chapter 7

UP SINCE SIX in the morning, Olivia had spent twelve hours on her keyboard. As anxious and resentful as Olivia felt—the aftermath of rehashing her exchanges with Catherine and experiences at Sullivan's—she managed to get in three chapters.

Engrossed in her writing, Olivia hadn't eaten lunch, had too many coffees inside her, and a massive headache drummed at her temples. Olivia needed to lay her head on her comfortable pillow and rest in complete darkness. So, it made perfect sense she was at Buzz's Bar with Sondra.

"How I let you talk me into this is beyond me?" Olivia rubbed at her temple.

The bar was packed with the after-work crowd. The seats ringing the bar were filled, as were all the tables. Flat screens around the room broadcasted the Blue Jays game, a cycling race, and women's volleyball. From the overhead speakers, By The Dashboard Light boomed over the murmur of conversation, laughter, and the cheers that broke out when Aaron Sanchez hit the ball out of the park. The smell of grilled meat scented the air, and servers carried trays of drinks and food to the tables.

"This is exactly what you need, not to be shut yourself in your empty house sulking." Sondra wore a black, slim-fitting dress similar to Olivia's and patent slingback shoes. Her hair, like Olivia's, spilled around a subtly painted face.

"For your information, I was writing all day." Olivia raised her voice over the cheering and music.

Sondra looked at Olivia with a raised brow. "As I said, sulking, but better to sulk at home than in the office."

"So, what's going on at the office?"

Sondra picked up her glass off the table and sipped on Cosmopolitan. "The same old bullshit. Vince is building his empire on Catherine's back and capitalizing on her stupidity. Elvira is riding on the high of her man's power because I can assure you she ain't riding on the high of his sexual prowess." Sondra flexed her pinky finger, and Olivia hooted a laugh.

"You and Oreo can always put a smile on my face."

"I'm at dog level. That is high praise." Sondra looked past Olivia and waved at the two men and the women with them at the bar.

"Damn straight it is." Olivia drank the last of her Cosmopolitan. "Who has taken over my accounts?"

"See, this," Sondra circled a finger at Olivia, "is what's wrong with you. Months after you left the company and you still care too much. You need to move on with your life, Olive Oyl."

"I was merely…."

"Here we go, ladies." Janie set Cosmopolitans in front of Sondra and Olivia and the family-size nacho platter at the centre of the table.

Janie had blue highlights running through her blonde hair. She wore pencil-tight jeans that accentuated shapely hips. Twenty-one-year-old ripe breasts spilled over the edge of a red, low-cut T-shirt just enough to tempt the men in the bar to open their wallets.

"You read my mind, Janie. Alcohol is exactly what Olivia needs. A few drinks in her, some nachos, and eye candy will wash away those depressing thoughts from her head." Sondra reached for her drink, tipped the glass to her lips, and drank deeply. With an approving cluck of her tongue, she said, "Nectar of the Gods."

Janie set down napkins and two packets of moist towelettes. "I'm here to make your life pleasurable. So just holler if you need anything."

"No need for that, Janie. Just keep the Cosmos coming every half hour, and from here on, make them doubles. Save you going back and forth because we aim to get drunk and lucky tonight." Sondra raised her glass in salute before she brought it to her lips.

"Good plan, ladies and by the way, I know most of the guys here. Let me know which ones you have your eye on, and I'll give you the four-one-one." Janie's dimples winked out of a wholesome, pretty face without much makeup.

"And that's why I demand to be sat at your section every time," Sondra said as tall, dark, and handsome strolled past their table. "That is yummy. Four-one-one, Janie."

"That's Geoff. He's in his mid-fifties, very single, and a cop. He has a uniform and handcuffs at his disposal," Janie said with a wicked wiggle of her eyebrows before she turned to pick up her next order at the bar.

"And they say men are sexist pigs." Olivia picked up her glass and drank sweet Cosmopolitan.

"That's a myth. Women are way worse than men." Sondra reached for a nacho. Hot, melted cheese stretched from the platter to her mouth. She wound the cheese string onto her finger and brought it to her mouth. "He's all yours."

"Who?"

"Mr. Policeman. Although I could teach him a thing or two, I'm twenty years younger and conceding him to you."

Olivia winged a brow. "Very gracious of you, but I'm not here to scout for a lay. I just want a drink and food and to chill." Olivia bit into a nacho loaded with melted cheese topped with a round of jalapeño pepper. "Oh, Jesus."

"How many times have I told you you're a jalapeño virgin and that you can't take a full round in one bite? You're beet-red now. How do you expect to reel in a roll in the sheets with Mr. Policeman looking like you're having a coronary?"

Olivia downed the remaining Cosmo in her glass in one swallow and chased it with the water Sondra handed her. "I have no interest in taking Mr. Policeman or anyone else home tonight." Oliva drew quick breaths as she fanned herself. "Sweet Jesus, that could kill a person."

"That right there is your problem, Olive Oyl."

"Being spiced to death is my problem?"

Cheers erupted as the Blue Jays brought a run in.

"That and the fact you're too uptight. What you need is a good lay. A good roll with a warm body never hurt anyone." Sondra tossed a jalapeño pepper into her mouth, chewed slowly, and savoured it. "And that's how you do it."

"All right, Spice Girl."

"Sleeping with a man is just sex. It doesn't mean marriage or commitment, as you old folks perceive it to be. Jesus, Olivia, we're in the twenty-first century."

Meatloaf segued into You Shook Me All Night Long, and the dance floor filled up.

"I have no interest in sex."

"You've gone so long without it that you're leading yourself to believe it. But mark my words, Olive Oyl, you get a taste again, and you're gonna want it all the time. Sex is part of our lifestyle, a bodily function necessary to sustain life."

Olivia lifted a single dark eyebrow when Sondra bit into another jalapeño round and didn't flinch. "Sustain life? Exaggerate much?"

Sondra smiled at Janie, who walked up with their Cosmo refill. "Tell my misguided friend how necessary sex is to a person."

"As necessary as the air we breathe." Janie set fresh drinks on the table and scooped up the empties. "I try to fill my lungs as often as possible. I can introduce you to Mr. Policeman."

"All right, stop it, you two." Olivia's rosy blush deepened.

"Mull it over, Olivia. I'll be back in half an hour." Janie headed toward the table of suits signalling for her.

"I bet you, Mr. Policeman, can loosen up that stress knotting your neck and shoulders. Why you let Catherine and her boy-toy get under your skin…."

"I thought Malcolm was joining us," Olivia interjected, hoping to steer the conversation in another direction.

"He'll be here later. Vince tossed a project on Malcolm's desk at the last minute and told him he needed it by tonight. As if dickhead and his blonde tart work Fridays."

"Who's allowing Vince to get under her skin now?"

"True that." Sondra tapped her glass to Olivia's and knocked her drink back. "To forgetting the fucktards in our lives."

Olivia drank to that. "By the way, you know Malcolm is eight years younger than you. He's young enough to…."

"Have his mind schooled in all that is Sondra? I have much to teach my young Jedi." Sondra's lips curved into a smile, and Olivia mirrored it. "Now, I bet you he doesn't need any schooling." Sondra tipped up her chin toward Mr. Policeman.

"On that, we are of mind equal." Olivia studied Mr. Policeman.

He was a tall glass of yum. His eyes, dove-gray, were set in a symmetrical, tanned face. His short, cropped hair was liberally salted at the temples, and he filled the black T-shirt and jeans nicely.

Olivia had to admit she liked what she saw.

Mr. Policeman would unknot her tightly wound tension. It had been way too long since she had her tension unwound or felt a man's arms around her, let alone have one in bed.

Olivia fixed blue eyes on Mr. Policeman and let her mind wander. He would definitely scratch the itch she needed scratching. He might even wash away her unhappiness—if for a night—but he couldn't fulfill her. No one and nothing fulfilled her anymore. Bob made sure of that.

Bob shattered her dreams and hopes and made it so she could never trust again. That, combined with the discontent with her life, exhausted any aspirations for a good relationship and life. Maybe it was midlife crises hitting. Whatever it was, Olivia was at an impasse, and she didn't know how to fix it.

She couldn't remember the last time she was happy. The once vibrant Olivia with the outgoing personality no longer existed. It had been so long since happiness had filled her that discontentment had become her permanent state of mind.

Writing made her happy, but for how long and where it led was yet to be seen. Olivia didn't know anything other than Sullivan's and the sales career she devoted her life to there. At her age, starting new was a gamble, and she had neither the time nor the energy or interest for innovation you have when young.

Olivia wanted a man in her life, someone to care for her, but settling wasn't an option at her age. She did that with Bob, and look how great that worked out.

Olivia wanted a friend, a partner, someone she could talk her day through with. She knew what it was like just to exist. She'd *existed* the entire time she was with Bob and wasn't returning to that.

To have a man who was more than average between the sheets wasn't too much to ask. For all his arrogance, Bob had been an average lover at best. But sex is an itch you scratch, it wasn't the entire basis of a good relationship. Olivia learned that the hard way, and she wanted the whole package and nothing but.

Olivia wanted a man with better-than-average bed skills who treated her as an equal, loved, and respected her. She could only be happy and fulfilled with such a man, and her search for the man who ticked all her boxes had become as challenging to find as the Holy Gail.

Olivia's eyes fixed on Mr. Policeman talking to Janie. In an unexpected move, his eyes flicked to Olivia and met hers. The admiring look he cast her drew an embarrassed smile from Olivia.

The panic set in Olivia when Mr. Policeman turned to head her way. "I think he's coming over."

Sondra stopped her drinking mid-sip. "Who?"

"Mr. Policeman." Panic shut off Olivia's air and crushed her chest. "What do I do?"

"Christ, woman, he's a man, one of the simplest species on this planet. Start with a hi. That should set things off. Follow that with the flutter of your lashes. Laugh at any stupid thing he says. Oh, and look interested when he talks." Sondra waved Malcolm over when she saw him walk into the bar. "Malcolm's here, so you're on your own."

Olivia's hand clamped down on Sondra's arm. "You're not leaving me to my own devices?"

"You're a grown-ass woman, Olivia." Sondra cast smiling eyes at Malcolm. "Hey, Malcolm." Her voice was as sweet as honey.

"S'up, Sondra." Malcolm's large, dark chocolate eyes in a bronze face lit with a smile.

He wore an intriguingly tight, white shirt that mapped out the hard chest and arms over skinny jeans. His beard was freshly trimmed, and there was the lingering scent of soap around him. "Don't you look and smell great?" Sondra breathed him in and decided he was getting lucky tonight. Where was yet to be determined.

"Thanks. You do too." Malcolm picked up a nacho and tossed it into his mouth.

Olivia stepped between Malcolm and Sondra. "I need a minute with Sondra, Malcolm."

"Oh, hey, Olivia."

"Yeah, whatever." Olivia batted Malcolm like a fly circling a plate of food.

"Rude," Malcolm said but stepped aside when Olivia shot death rays at him.

"Sit, Malcolm," Olivia commanded. He did. "You got me into this, and you're not leaving me to sink. Sit." The cold, steely glint in Olivia's blue eyes had Sondra falling back on the chair. "You think I missed the head nod you gave Janie? Was it the go-ahead to get Mr. Policeman to come over?"

"Maybe." Sondra huffed a breath when Olivia's mouth clamped in a long, firm line. "Yeah, I did. So, what? Maybe you'll get some tonight. And believe you me, you need it."

"Way to go, Olivia." Malcolm gave her the thumbs up sign.

Olivia never took her eyes off Sondra. "Shoo, Malcolm. Go get yourself a drink at the bar," Olivia said, and he hurried off.

"You come right back, Malcolm," Sondra called out over Olivia's shoulder. "You're misaligning my chi, woman."

"How many times have I told you…?"

"Hello, Mr. Policeman," Sondra said, pasting a smile on her face.

Up close, Mr. Policeman was taller and more handsome. "Hi."

"I'm Sondra, and this is my very single friend, Olivia." Sondra spun Olivia around to face Mr. Policeman.

Colour flooded Olivia's face.

"That's a pretty name, Olivia. I'm Geoff."

"And that's my cue to exit." Sondra walked away.

"Nice to meet you," Olivia said with an even tone.

Karaoke night was launched with a bad rendition of Madonna's Like A Virgin, sung by a platinum-blond, curvy woman cheered by her friends.

Loud cheers went up when platinum-blond Madonna claimed to be touched for the first time and seductively traced a hand over her curvy hip.

"I'd say she's Madonna's doppelgänger," Geoff said.

Geoff looked fit, and his body solid Olivia swallowed hard. "Yes, difficult to tell the two apart. I'm sorry about my friend."

"Don't be. Everyone has a Sondra. Mine is Todd, and he'll say whatever comes to mind without consulting his brain first." Geoff's smile sharpened. "Can I refill your drink, Olivia?"

"Sure, thank you."

The night stretched out ahead of them in perfect harmony. Olivia and Geoff drank, ate, and enjoyed one another's company. Her headache miraculously gone, Olivia joined Geoff on the stage for karaoke when Sondra, Malcolm, Janie, and Geoff's friends spurred them. Singing Island In The Stream, he was her Kenny, and she his Dolly.

"I'm sorry, but I have to get going. I wish I didn't, but I have an early shift tomorrow." Geoff was pleased to see the disappointment in her eyes. "I had a great time tonight."

"Me too."

"Can I, um, maybe call you?" Geoff's question sent her heart racing. Olivia wondered if he heard it thudding as hard as it was.

"I'd like that." The silence drifted between them for a while. "I'm not sure how this works. Do you give me your number, or do I give you mine?"

"How about I give you my number, and you call me back, so it shows up on my call log?"

"That works." Olivia reached into her handbag for her cell phone and saw the dozen missed calls from Mount Sinai Hospital. The last two were from her sister. She felt a thump of panic.

"Is everything okay?"

"I'm not sure. Give me a minute." Olivia dialled Lottie's number. "What's wrong, Lottie?" Olivia held the phone inches from her ear when Lottie began to scream. "I know. I'm sorry I missed your calls. I couldn't hear the ringing phone. I'm in a... Never mind. What's wrong?"

"You need to get to the hospital," Lottie said.

Olivia's heart was in her throat. "Why? Are the girls okay? Are you? Is it Ken?" Olivia listened to Lottie with Geoff watching on. "Oh, is that all? Why call me, and how did they get a hold of you."

"They said you're his emergency contact, and when they couldn't get a hold of you, they somehow got my number and called me."

"Why?"

"They wouldn't tell me anything. Just get to the hospital, Olivia. It sounds urgent," Lottie said.

"Since when have you cared about Bob?"

"Never, but it sounded urgent. Maybe he's dying and wants to let you know he's leaving his worldly possessions to you."

Olivia recognized sarcasm when she heard it. "I don't care if he's on his death bed."

"You picked him. He's your ex. Deal with it, Olivia. I don't want them calling me again."

"Fine, which hospital?" Olivia hung up.

"Everything okay?" asked Geoff.

"I'm sorry, but I have to go." Olivia turned to Malcolm. "I need you to drive me to Mount Sinai Hospital."

"Why me?" Malcolm was rounding third base with Sondra, and it was a matter of time before he crossed home plate.

"Because Sondra's floating on happy."

"Yes, I know." Malcolm flashed Olivia a wicked smile.

"Yeah, okay. Olivia gathered her things and tossed a few bills on the table. You don't drink."

"And…"

"Christ, can't anyone just do one thing I ask." Olivia huffed a breath. "Do I need to spell it out, Malcolm? You're the only one who hasn't had a drink all night and can get behind the wheel. Now, Malcolm. Don't make me wallop you."

"You're bossy and violent. You know we're not at the office."

"No, because if we were, Vince would be directing you not to help me out because you're his bitch," Olivia said between gritted teeth.

"Oh, wow, is that necessary? I confide in you, and you throw it in my face."

"Sondra, get your things. You're coming for the ride. Malcolm can drop me off at the hospital, and the two of you can go on to perform the acrobatic acts you've been intimating at all night."

"I can get behind that," Malcolm said with a grin that Sondra echoed.

Olivia slung her handbag over her shoulder. "I'm sorry, Geoff. Gotta go."

"What happened? Who's in the hospital?" Sondra chased after Olivia.

"It's Bob," Olivia called over her shoulder.

"Who's Bob?" Geoff asked Malcolm.

"Olivia's husband."

"You mean ex-husband," Geoff said.

"Nope, still husband. You dodged a bullet there, buddy. The woman is a hand-grenade." Malcolm's fingers burst open in an explosive gesture. "Well, nice meeting you, dude." Malcolm walked around a dazed Geoff.

Chapter 8

MALCOLM STOPPED HIS SUV in front the hospital's emergency department. A good friend, Sondra, offered to stay with Olivia. To Sondra's relief, Olivia turned the offer down. Bob was Olivia's husband, her responsibility. Besides, if Olivia were the reason for Sondra's missed opportunity to show Malcolm her bendable talent, she'd hold it over her head for eternity. Olivia would sooner burn in the fires of hell than have to deal with that scenario.

Walking through the sliding doors, the universal smell of antiseptic and despair slapped Olivia. In the waiting room, a baby wailed, and his mother rocked and shushed him with her husband helplessly looking on. An old man helped his trembling wife to her feet a few chairs over. A group of teenagers huddled in the corner, tapping on their phones while their friend sat in a wheelchair writhing in pain. Others read or watched the news on the television hanging from the wall as they awaited to see a doctor.

"Excuse me, I'm looking for Bob Huntley," Olivia said to the receptionist behind the desk.

Her flaming red hair was tied in a loose ponytail. Tendrils spilled around the unpainted youthful face. She wore a flower print shirt and black pants that emitted a strong scent of laundry detergent.

Red looked up at Olivia. "Are you family?"

Olivia nodded. "I'm his wife, Olivia Fal ... Huntley." Red looked at Olivia silently for a moment. Olivia could see her thinking. "Sorry, I mainly go by my maiden name these days."

Red gave her a knowing look. "Just a moment, Mrs. Huntley."

It had been long since she'd been addressed as Mrs. Huntley. Effortlessly Olivia slid into the past, to her first real kiss and the boy she'd shared it with—George.

George was the only boy who gave an overweight, awkward, unpopular, insecure girl attention, and Olivia was grateful.

It started as a bump-into encounter in the hallway and progressed into sharing a study table in the library. That led to pizza and a movie one month later. Six weeks on, George made a move to kiss Olivia.

The scene rolled into Olivia's mind as vividly as if it was yesterday.

They sat on the bench overlooking the lake. A full moon rode white over the dark water of the lake, leaving a trail of light in its path. The music from cicadas poured into the night, and the air was ripe with the rich summer scents of heat and the smell of George's cheap cologne. Olivia smelled it now.

Bonnie Tyler sang passionately about a total eclipse of the heart from the radio of a parked car where young love was being forged. To this day, when Olivia heard the song, her mind took her back to that moment.

The kiss was awkward and lasted seconds, but it turned Olivia's world on its axis. That kiss changed Olivia's outlook on life and herself, and she was never the same.

Amazing how one simple act can make such an indelible impression on your life.

Olivia's confidence soared. She started running and lost the excess weight. She replaced glasses with contacts, and her wardrobe went from shabby frumpy to chic.

Olivia and George eventually became an item, inseparable until—

Olivia ordered herself not to think about it. Now wasn't the time to walk back through a past she couldn't correct.

"Your husband has gone up to imaging, Mrs. Huntley." Bob's chart in hand, Red swung her swivel chair and wheeled back to her desk. "He should be down in thirty minutes. You can wait in the waiting room." Red pointed to the room across the reception desk.

"Thank you. I'll do that. By the way, what's Bob in for? We've been estranged for some time, and I haven't seen him in a while. I don't know why he'd put me down as his emergency contact." Olivia explained when Red's brow creased in a frown.

Sisterly understanding flashed in Red's eyes, and she industriously pecked on the keyboard and accessed Bob's file. "Mr. Huntley has an inoperable brain tumour called a glioblastoma multiforme."

The shock flew into Olivia's eyes. "Christ! Are you sure?"

"I'm sorry, Mrs. Huntley. He suffered a heart attack and was out when brought in."

The thumping in Olivia's head returned. The sound of nurses and doctors coming and going, the shrill of an ambulance siren, beeping monitors, the announcements blaring over the PA system, and the moaning patients drummed in Olivia's head.

"Are you all right, Mrs. Huntley?"

"I'm fine," Olivia said, although she stared, shock glazing her eyes.

"Can I get you a glass of water?"

Olivia shook her head. "How bad is it?"

"I've already given you too much information. You'll have to speak to Dr. Papa, Mr. Huntley's neurologist. He'll answer all of your questions. I'll page him. Have a seat in the waiting room. I'll come to get you when the doctor gets in."

Flummoxed, Olivia drew back from the desk. "All right, thank you." She took a couple of steps and then turned around. "Is it all right if I step out for a few minutes? I need to get some air?"

"Go ahead. Dr. Papa won't be here for a while." Red turned her attention to the ringing cell phone.

Chapter 9

STANDING OUTSIDE, UNDER the canopy of the emergency entrance, Olivia breathed cool night air. The rain had come and gone all night. It pelted the city, a sheet of rain that fell thick and hard. Olivia could smell the woody aroma of watered soil. White light from lampposts reflected off the wet pavement. But for the few cars in the visitor parking lot. It was nearly empty.

Olivia reached into her handbag for the cell phone when it pinged. It was a text from Lottie. *Hey, you ok? What's going on?*

Olivia texted back: *I'm good. Waiting to see Bob.*

Do U want me to come to keep U company? Adam can stay with the kids.

No need both of us sitting around for hours.

K. Text me anytime if U want to talk or want company.

Will do. Get some sleep.

Lottie texted back a smiley face.

Sipping bad machine dispensed coffee, Olivia watched the EMTs, a man and woman in yellow reflective coats, roll the stretcher from the back of the ambulance. The passed-out man on the stretcher was wrapped in a white sheet, and his black, clean-shaven face and bald, shiny head were all visible. As they wheeled past Olivia, she caught a closer glimpse of the red-stained sheet resulting from a gunshot wound.

Olivia looked away and stared at the black sky.

After the long day, Olivia's system signalled to shut down, but her day was only beginning. She sipped on lousy coffee to ward off the effect of alcohol taking over.

So many questions crowded her head.

How did she come to be Bob's emergency contact? It had been twenty-five years since they last spoke. Twenty-five years since he disappeared overnight, leaving her with so much debt, she thought she'd never surface to see another bright day.

Bob mortgaged the home where she and her sister grew up and entrusted to Olivia weeks before her father died.

Olivia blamed no one but herself for trusting Bob and signing the documents he put in front of her without question. It wasn't until he left her she found out about the mortgages he took on her home.

Why call her now? Olivia was his wife on paper, but they were long estranged. She was the woman he didn't contact once after he left. Olivia suspected Bob didn't contact her because of the debts he left, but because she'd ask him to pay for the divorce, she would push on him.

Bob vanished like a puff of smoke. Without money to spare for a private investigator or lawyers, Olivia gave up looking for him. Besides, what was she going to do if she found him? She didn't have the money to pay for the divorce she knew Bob wouldn't pay for. Years later, when she had the funds for the divorce, it wasn't a priority. It had been so long since she'd heard from Bob that for all Olivia knew, he was dead.

Olivia didn't plan to marry ever again.

After Bob, trust in men was difficult for Olivia. Nothing made Olivia happy, and nothing fulfilled her but work and surviving and paying off the debts was her sole focus. In the end, working filled the man-less hole in her life, and work drove her and fulfilled her.

Why would Bob turn to her now, decades later?

At fifty-five, Bob was likely shacking up with a girl half his age. The man hated to be alone.

The doors to the Emergency Department slid open. Through them walked the woman she'd seen in the waiting room cradling the baby in her arms. The wave of fatigue washing over her face was visible in the shadowed eyes. The woman in her twenties trailing her walked through the doors and stood opposite Olivia. She took a pack of cigarettes from her shirt pocket, shook one out, and sucked it to life.

She had long blonde hair that fountained around a delicate, youthful face with moss green eyes. She wore faded jeans, a tattered brown sweater, and running shoes that had seen much use. In designer labels, Olivia could see Red on the cover of fashion magazines.

"Would you like one?" She offered Olivia the pack. Olivia shook her head. "Don't smoke?"

"Never have."

"I wish I'd never started. Hard to quit now, you know." She tapped away cigarette ash. "One positive, it helps keep my weight down. I'm Cassie Nash."

"Olivia." Succinct, but Olivia wasn't in the mood to indulge in conversation.

Cassie watched Olivia fuel herself with coffee. "It's really, really bad, isn't it?"

Olivia gently nodded for fear of making her head feel worse.

"Then why drink it?" Cassie sighed out smoke.

Conversation was unavoidable, and Olivia said, "I need the caffeine."

Cassie studied Olivia through the haze of smoke. "Too much partying?"

A deep sigh escaped Olivia. "I was out with a friend who always manages to make me go astray."

"My friend's like that. That's why I'm here. His friends talked him into drinking too much whiskey, and out of nowhere, he passed out." Cassie snapped her fingers.

"I'm sorry to hear. I hope he's okay." Olivia rubbed at her temple, hoping to relieve the pressure in her head.

"I have some aspirin if you like." Cassie reached into her bag.

"Thanks. I took a couple not long ago."

"Oh, okay. Well, I have it if you need it. I have to carry it with me everywhere I go for my friend. He has a bad heart." Cassie pitched the cigarette on the ground. "Much good it did tonight, though. He had a heart attack right there in front of me. I pop the pills into his mouth, and nothing."

"I'm sorry to hear, but I think you take aspirin to prevent the heart attack."

Cassie's big green eyes puzzled. "Are you sure? I've seen on TV where they pop them into their mouth, and poof, they're better."

"I think you're thinking of Nitroglycerin."

"Nitro, who?"

"Nitroglycerin is what you pop under someone's mouth when they have a heart attack."

"Shit, you're right. How do you know all this?"

"They write it in books."

"You think I'm stupid."

Olivia looked taken aback. "No, I don't. You just need to be educated on the topic."

Cassie knew that was true, and her gaze was full of understanding when it lifted. "You're right, but why would my friend tell me to carry aspirin with me?"

"I'm not sure. You should ask him."

Cassie sucked on the cigarette she fired to life. "I don't think I'll be able to. They say he had a massive heart attack. Right there, in front of me, he had a heart attack. It freaked me out, you know. Then he screams at me to call 9-1-1. All the way here, in the ambulance, when he could get a word out, from under the oxygen mask, he's screaming at me." She sucked some more smoke and exhaled. "He's always screaming lately. Sometimes, he gets mean. Not handsy. He's not like that. He gets verbal. Christ does he ever, and I don't know how to respond."

The subtext of the conversation was there, and Olivia said, "You don't have to put up with that. Not from your friend, not from anyone."

"I know, but I can't leave him. He's dependent on me."

"Of course, you can. I speak from experience when I tell you that you should stop it before it's too late. Nothing good will come from staying with him."

Cassie lowered her gaze. "He has a brain tumour. He says it's mal ... mal...."

"Malignant." Olivia finished when Cassie struggled with the word.

"Yeah, that's it. He's lost his sight because of the tumour, and it makes him crazy sometimes. I mean, it would make me crazy too if I couldn't see anymore." Cassie tossed down her cigarette and ground it out with the tip of her shoe. "He says he doesn't have much time, maybe a one month, two."

In the ensuing silence, it hit Olivia like a hand grenade.

Cassie anticipated the question before it was asked. "Yes, Bob's my … friend. I know who you are, Olivia."

Olivia was still as stone.

Lightning split the sky and lit it bright. Seconds later, Thunder exploded. Clouds heavy with rain burst and more rain poured.

"I get confused like the aspirin and Nitroglycerin thing, and I can't make decisions. He says I'm useless. That's why he put you down as his emergency contact." Cassie's green eyes were locked on Olivia, who remained quiet, drinking coffee to moisten her dry mouth. "He said you're still married, and as his wife, you can make decisions for him. You know the doctors ask a lot of questions. Like really important questions, and I can't give them answers. I'm too stupid."

"You're not stupid," was Olivia's automatic response. She knew exactly how Bob's tongue cut, debased and humiliated. "You're not stupid."

"Thanks." Cassie's mouth lifted at one corner. "He needs your help. I need your help."

A thirty-ish couple, the wife grunted and caressed her football-shaped belly as her panicked husband held an umbrella over her to shield her from the rain, ambled past them and through the sliding door.

"How long have you been with Bob?" Olivia asked.

"Three years. I'm older than I look. I'm twenty-one," Cassie said.

They were getting younger and younger, Olivia thought, studying Cassie. In Cassie's moss-green eyes, Oliva saw a naïve child seduced by a man's unutterable maleness and charisma with the gift of the gab.

She'd been where Cassie was and understood Bob's appeal and his pull on a woman. He knew the right words to say and things to whisper in a woman's ear to seduce her to bed.

Olivia knew because once, long ago, she was Cassie.

Olivia also knew Bob's charm only worked on youthful innocence, not a woman who'd experienced life as she had.

"I know he wasn't very nice to you, Olivia. He told me all about it. You know how it is when you're close to death and want to unburden yourself." She pulled another cigarette out of the pack and lit it with the one burning between her fingers. "I imagine you really must hate him. I would, but he needs you right now. I know it's a lot to ask, Olivia," Cassie lifted the eyes, young and vulnerable, "but will you help him?"

The air hummed between them for a while.

"I know you don't know me, but will you help me? I can't do this on my own." Cassie's pleading eyes stared at Olivia.

Olivia shut her eyes for a moment. That hard line between what was, what is fused, and only the present existed. At that instant, Olivia could only nod.

Part II

The Middle

Forgiveness is the ultimate expression of kindness—to yourself.

—M.L. Lexi

Chapter 10

TOO MANY FEELINGS, too many thoughts tumbled around Olivia's head. She needed time alone to let the shock of the night wash through her system, and she said to Cassie, "Why don't you go get us drinkable coffee? There should be a twenty-four-hour coffee shop nearby?"

"Sure, okay, but I don't have a car. I came in the ambulance with Bob. I'm a good driver, have a license, and won't take off with your car," Cassie added when she saw Olivia studying her in silence through the haze of cigarette smoke.

"It's not that."

"Promise, I'll drive real carefully." After some consideration, Olivia hesitantly handed Cassie her car keys.

"I don't, ah, have any money."

Olivia fished a twenty-dollar bill from her handbag. "It's the black SUV to the right of the parking lot entrance."

"I'll find it."

Olivia watched Cassie walk toward the parking lot, pointing and clicking the key fob until the car beeped before she turned to head inside.

On her way to the waiting room, Olivia saw Red behind her desk. The cell phone was cradled on her shoulder as she typed on the computer's keyboard. When Red saw Olivia, she shook her head to indicate she had no information on Bob. Olivia continued to the waiting room.

The waiting room was empty and small. The smell of paint from the freshly painted pastel-blue walls hung in the air. Gray vinyl chairs lined three walls with tables at each corner displaying a selection of out-of-date magazines. A flat-screen television on the facing wall aired the weather report. Thunderstorms and rain were to persist until late morning.

Olivia sat facing the window. Rain pattered against the windowpane, a soothing drumming. Outside of the waiting room, the hubbub of hospital sounds resonated.

Drained in emotion, she threw back her head and shut her tired eyes. She had come full circle with Bob. And in typical Bob fashion, he re-entered Olivia's life at a vulnerable time to disrupt it. If that wasn't enough, Bob inserts his twenty-one-year-old blonde bed warmer into the equation.

Olivia's phone pinged, and she reached into her handbag.

Hey, babe, checking in. Are u ok? Read the text from Sondra.

Tired, but ok. Still waiting to see Bob.

Why is the f-tard bothering you after all this time?

Olivia imagined Sondra's fingers typing at angry speed accompanied by an oath-laced rant aimed at Bob, whom she'd never met, but had heard so much about.

Long story, lots to tell. What's going on with u?

Malcolm didn't need much teaching after all. Smiley face.

TMI

LOL. What's wrong with f-tard?

TMI for a text. It's more of a liquid lunch convo.

Do you want me to come n keep u company?

No, I'm good. Thx.

Thank u for talking Malcolm into leaving his car for me to use and Ubering home.

Already have 2x.

Christ woman, TMI.

LOL. I didn't want u Ubering home alone late at night.

Awww, U care.

Course I do Olive Oyl.

Get back to your sordid night.

Twist my arm. I'm here for u babe. Text me anytime. Just not in the next 20 minutes. Will be busy.

Ewww. Heart u.

LOL. Heart u back.

Olivia returned the cell phone to her handbag as Cassie walked into the waiting room with two coffees on a tray and a food bag. Olivia tilted her eyes up to look at her. For the storm of emotions assailing her, Olivia showed nothing. It was two o'clock in the morning, and she was too tired and feeling the aftermath of six double Cosmopolitans.

"I hope you don't mind. I picked up food to ward off your hangover." Cassie jiggled the cup off the tray and handed it to Olivia.

Olivia folded the lid tab, locked it in place, and took a swig of coffee. "Christ, that's good coffee," she said, kicking her shoes off and arching her feet.

"Almost forgot." Cassie fished the car keys from her jeans pocket and turned them and the leftover change from her purchase to Olivia. "That's a nice ride you have."

"Thanks." Olivia imagined what Bob drove if Malcolm's no-frills SUV inspired Cassie.

"Donut, muffin, or chicken wrap?" Cassie asked. "I can eat either. I'm starving."

Olivia shook her head. "You go ahead. I'm not hungry." She was starving, but her stomach was doing cartwheels, and she didn't think she could keep food down.

The mere idea of coming face-to-face with Bob after all these years wasn't reason for celebration. After the anger, the hate, and the resentment, after mending her shattered heart and dignity, she'd set him to the back of her mind and hadn't given him a second thought.

Bob had stolen so much from Olivia. He stole her faith in humanity, her confidence, and her self-respect. For the longest time, Olivia blamed herself for what Bob did to her. She allowed Bob into her life and permitted him to do what he had. She chose Bob over George because he could give her what George couldn't.

Or that's what George had led her to believe.

George was the son of the school custodian, whereas Bob was the son of a renowned lawyer and proprietor of the long-established Huntley & Associates LLP. Olivia met Bob at nineteen when she applied to Huntley & Associates for the receptionist position to earn money for her university tuition.

One year older than Olivia, Bob was studying to become a lawyer to one day step into his dad's shoes, take over the firm, and carry his legacy.

That's what Bob told Olivia when he proposed marriage after their third date.

The appeal to become the wife of a soon-to-be lawyer and owner of a profitable firm was too good for Olivia to pass up. Olivia willingly gave up university, her plans, and her dreams for Bob. Robert Huntley Jr's wife would not hold down a job, was what Bob told her.

Olivia could still see the shock on George's face when she told him she'd accepted Bob's marriage proposal.

"I didn't know you were interested in marriage. I mean, you're nineteen." George crouched down beside Olivia on the grass.

"Neither was I." Olivia's eyes welled up.

Except for the sound of Olivia weeping, the park she and George often met at was quiet and peaceful. The smell of grass and fall wafted all around them.

"You barely know Bob." George stretched out his jeans-clad legs and crossed his feet at the ankles.

Olivia wiped at her tears. "He says he loves me." She wore jeans and an oversized maroon sweatshirt, and her long, dark hair spilled around her face that needed no make-up.

"I thought we were getting along." George wanted to punch the elm tree supporting their backs. Despite himself, he stroked his hand down her hair in a casually intimate way. "I thought we really liked each other."

"We were, and I do like you, but that's just it, George. It's like. In the months we've dated, you never once said you love me, George."

In pure frustration, George dragged a hand through his hair and rose to pace. She could see his huffed breaths in the cold air. "I know, but we're young."

"That doesn't mean you can't say the words, George."

"You don't understand, Olivia." George knelt before her. "It's not that I can't say the words."

"It's that you don't want to. What's the difference?"

George's eyes cut away from hers. "That's not it, Olivia."

The hurt clear on her face, she rose to her feet. "Well, you don't have to worry about it anymore, George. I'm marrying Bob."

And Olivia did.

The vows said Bob and Olivia made a home in the basement of her father's house. It wasn't until then that Olivia found out why Bob was rushing to marry her.

"Mrs. Huntley." Olivia looked up to meet Red's eyes. "Mr. Huntley is back from imaging and has been set up in a room. You can see him now."

"All right, thank you." She and Cassie simultaneously rose to their feet.

"I'm sorry, but I can only allow family and one at a time," said Red.

"This is Cassie, our, ah, daughter. I know he'd like to see her," Olivia stammered. She doubted Red believed the lie, but the last thing she wanted was to walk into Bob's room alone.

Red's frown line deepened momentarily between her eyebrows. Olivia and Red looked at each other for a moment.

"Please," Olivia pled.

"Room 425, on the fourth floor."

Olivia felt her stomach muscles knotting.

Chapter 11

OLIVIA CAUGHT HER breath, and there was a tightening in her chest. Frozen on the spot, she remained arched in the doorway of Bob's room, unable to take another step. Olivia stared for a long while without speaking. When the haze cleared from Olivia's mind, she felt limp.

Not the way Olivia expected the encounter to go, but it was a surreal moment.

Machines, their wires stemming from various parts of Bob's body, beeped and recorded data. The six-foot, two-hundred-pound man with the imposing presence, was a shell of the person Olivia knew. He'd lost half his weight and the crown of thick dark hair. His brown eyes, sunk deep in their socket, were shadowed with despair. He looked frail and as pale as the bedsheet that covered him.

She found something she didn't expect—empathy, sadness, compassion?—unexpectedly rising in her.

To think this was the overbearing, controlling man she came to resent and hate. Bob stole her dignity, her confidence, and her love for life. He coarsened her soul. Now, he was a mere shell of himself.

How many times had she wished him the worst? How many times had she damned Bob? How many times had she regretted meeting and having him in her life?

How much time had she spent hating and resenting?

Now, all Olivia could do was feel sorry for Bob.

Olivia watched Cassie walk up to Bob's bed. "Hi." She reached for his hand and held it between hers. "Feeling better?"

"I am, baby." Bob's voice was low and weak. "Is she here?"

"She is. Olivia's standing by the doorway, to your right," Cassie said.

Bob's eyes remained looking straight ahead. "Hello, Olivia."

"Hello, Bob," Olivia said in a tone that blended cheerfulness and sympathy.

"You look good, Olivia," Bob said quietly before he burst out laughing. "Sorry, some dark humour on my part. You see, I've gone blind."

How did you respond to that? I'm sorry, seemed like a cliché response, and you too look good boorish. Why was it you became tongue-tied in situations where words mattered?

Olivia settled for, "Thank you."

"Good one," Cassie chimed in with a snorting giggle when his eyes turned morose. "But she does look great. She's very pretty."

Bob's eyes narrowed and focused on the silhouette by the door to get a glimpse of her, but he saw only blurry darkness. "Water, Cassie," Bob said, licking his lips.

Cassie brought a Styrofoam cup with a straw from the night table and held it to Bob's thin, dry lips. Bob struggled for breath between the tiny sips of water.

Olivia watched Cassie reach for a tissue and wipe the drool from Bob's mouth. The ball of pity lodged in Olivia's throat.

"Sorry about the drooling, but it's how it is now. I'm sure you're enjoying this, Olivia."

Olivia cleared her throat and took a step forward. "That's not at all the case, Bob. I'm sorry this happened to you."

"Don't apologize, Olivia, and don't feel sorry for me. I don't want your sympathy." Bob struggled to take another few drops of water.

"Ignore him. It's the anger talking." Cassie mouthed at Olivia and then turned to prop Bob's pillows.

"Stop fussing, Cassie," Bob snapped.

Cassie's head sank forward, and she tucked her hands into her jeans pocket. "Sorry, I just want to make you comfortable."

"Where's Olivia?" Bob struggled to sit up in bed. "Honey, raise the back of the bed a bit."

Jekyll and Hyde, Olivia thought.

Cassie waved Olivia in, and she walked closer to Bob's bed but still left a foot of distance between them.

Light spilled around Bob from the wall-mounted strip behind his bed. Up close, he looked worse, like a live corpse. Olivia could hear him wheeze, struggling to breathe. She pressed her hand to her belly as it roiled.

"She's to your right," Cassie said, and he turned his head.

"Thank you for coming, Olivia. I know this can't be easy for you. Has Cassie filled you in on why you're here?"

"She has." Olivia's voice shook, broke.

"I must be a sight. I apologize, but chemo, meds, and lack of appetite tend to wear a body down." His voice was thin and shaky.

"I'm sorry," she said, as much as it didn't have the right tenor for the moment.

"No need for apologies, Olivia." Bob signalled for more water. Cassie obliged by guiding the straw to his thin lips and patiently held it while he struggled to take a couple of sips. "Thank you, darling." He turned to Olivia. "If anyone should apologize, Olivia, it's me to you for everything I did. You didn't deserve any of it. I was an asshole and blind to it."

They shared a silence.

"I'm not looking for forgiveness, Olivia. It's just something I needed to say to you before…. You'd be surprised how introspective you become when death's knocking at your door."

Olivia didn't say anything. The silence became increasingly palpable.

"Cassie, will you give Olivia and me a minute?"

"Yeah, sure. I'm due for a cigarette. Yes, quitting is on my to-do list. I promise," Cassie said when Bob's brow winged. She kissed Bob and stepped out of the room.

"I am sorry, Olivia, for hurting you. For not being the man you deserved, for lying, for the debt I left you to carry. For everything. Christ, I was such an asshole. It's too bad your eyes aren't open wide to the person you are until you're at death's door. Water," Bob said when his voice strained, and he started to cough.

Olivia moved to pick up the Styrofoam glass and brought it to his lips.

"Thank you," Bob said after a strained sip and laboured swallow. "

"I know I can't make it up to you and that this apology falls into the too-little-too-late category, but it's all I can give you." Olivia brought the straw to Bob's mouth. "I don't know if Cassie mentioned it, but I need your help, Olivia."

Olivia walked to the window. It was approaching two in the morning. At this time of night, the silence merged with the darkness. University Avenue was devoid of the heavy traffic that would fill it in a few hours. The heavy rain had abated to a drizzle. Under the glow of streetlamps, the wet streets glistened. "She mentioned something."

"Cassie's a wonderful girl, but she's, shall we say, green."

"If by that you mean more than half your age, I can't argue with you there."

Bob burst out in a laugh that segued into a coughing fit. Olivia gave him water. "I wish you had that sharp tongue when we were together. It might have set me straight."

"Doubt it. You were a grade A...."

"Fuckwad, fucktard, ginormous asshole, I know that now," Bob injected when Olivia hesitated.

"I had other adjectives in mind, but those suit fine."

"You always did have a good sense of humour." Bob gave her a shaky laugh. "I'd understand if you don't want to help me, Olivia, and I wouldn't blame you, but will you? As my wife, you have absolute power to make decisions for me, medically, financially, and otherwise, when I'm no longer able to."

Olivia took in some long, quiet breaths. "What about your family, your sister, your mother and your father?"

"Mom and Dad passed away a few years back."

"I'm sorry. I didn't know."

"As for my sister, I burned that bridge long ago. She refuses to allow me to be a part of her life or her family's, and rightly so."

"I'm sure if your sister knew your, ah, situation, she'd let bygones be bygones."

"You haven't. You pity me, but you can't forgive me."

"I…"

He raised a limp hand. "As I said, I'm not asking for your forgiveness, Olivia. I don't deserve it. What I'm asking for is your help." Olivia couldn't find the words for a minute until he said, "Please, Olivia. I don't have much time. I know you better than I know anyone that's been in my life. You're my longest relationship. I trust you to make the right decisions for me. I'm desperate, Olivia. I need your help. Please, will you help me?"

Olivia thought about that for a moment. She had a lot on her plate then. She was unemployed and, worse, unemployable. She had limited funds to survive and needed to get her book written to generate an income. The turmoil and pressure of caring for a dying man would affect her serenity and clog up her mind, which wouldn't be conducive to writing her book.

And what did Bob mean by making decisions for him financially and otherwise? Was there a risk of him saddling her with debt?

Oliva regretted not pursuing the divorce when she had the chance.

Olivia thought of Cassie. She was ill-equipped and too young to care for a dying man, but Cassie wasn't her responsibility. Cassie should have known what she was getting into when she became involved with a man twice her age, Olivia told herself.

Olivia gave the situation some thought. She didn't know what she got herself into when she married Bob, Olivia countered in her head.

Olivia swallowed heavily. "I can't do this, Bob."

A slow smile formed on Bob's lips. "But you will."

Shaking her head, Olivia said, "Yes, I will."

Chapter 12

IT WAS TWO a.m. when Olivia left the hospital. Traffic was light, and Olivia was grateful for that. Hungover and mentally drained from the worst day of her life, she needed to get home and into bed before the new day began. Olivia had a lot on her plate today.

In four hours, she had to drive to Malcolm's place to pick up Sondra and him and head to Buzz's Bar, where her car sat on the lot.

Next on Olivia's TO-DO list was to contact her lawyer. Olivia needed to pose the inevitable question of how to swiftly sever her marriage to Bob to avoid any possible financial repercussions he may bring her way. Olivia had worked too hard to do an about-turn in her life.

Olivia had to put in a call to Dr. Papa, who didn't show up last night. Called into emergency surgery on arrival at the hospital, Oliva didn't get the opportunity to speak to him about Bob's prognosis.

Red told Olivia that Dr. Papa was the top neurologist in the country, and there was some comfort in that. No matter how horrible a husband Bob was throughout their marriage, and as much as Olivia wished him pain, he didn't deserve such a miserable death.

Olivia needed to schedule a face-to-face meeting with Dr. Papa. She needed to meet the man caring for Bob and ask the hundreds of questions she had.

Olivia made every green light and was home in thirty minutes. Her loyal, loving boy greeted her at the front door with a bark of happiness that she was home.

"Hi, Oreo. I'm sorry, I'm so late, bud." Olivia tossed her coat and handbag onto the foyer bench, and both missed the mark and fell onto the tiled floor. She left it there. "I had a full night, and I'm shattered." Olivia kicked her shoes off, walked into the living room, and fell face down onto the couch. Oreo jumped up and lay next to her.

Sleep came quickly for both.

Deep in sleep, Olivia's dreams were filled with images of Bob's fragile, deteriorating body. His lifeless eyes stared at her as he lay in a mahogany casket. The images in Olivia's subconscious evolved into her standing under a dark sky, a wall of rain coming down on her as she stared down where Bob's coffin lay deep in the ground. Olivia saw thousands of maggots wriggle their way into the coffin.

With a jolt, Olivia came out of sleep.

The clock on the mantel read five-thirty.

Catching her breath, Olivia wiped the sleep out of her eyes. Her mouth was bone dry, and her head felt like it would split any minute. Pushing off the couch and around Oreo, Olivia walked to the kitchen and poured herself a glass of water. From the pantry, she fished the Tylenol bottle.

Chasing two Tylenol pills with water, Olivia walked to the kitchen table and fired up her laptop. She typed glioblastoma multiforme tumour into the search bar.

Olivia read as much as she could.

"Christ," she murmured under her breath when she read it was one of the most aggressive types of cancer.

Surgery wasn't an option to remove the tumour, she read. Olivia reached for pen and paper, made notes, and wrote questions to ask Dr. Papa when she met with him.

There were different stages of glioblastoma multiforme tumours, Olivia wrote. Stage four was the worst and the stage Olivia deduced Bob was at. She made a notation to confirm with the doctor.

Olivia noted the treatments available per the Mayo Clinic's website. She would discuss Bob's options with Dr. Papa. The symptoms that affected glioblastoma patients were mood swings, loss of balance and memory, along with loss of appetite, which was evident in the muscular body that wasn't anymore. Other symptoms were nausea, vomiting, and speech challenges, followed by death. Olivia's throat went tight, and she pressed her fingers to her eyes.

Coffee, Olivia thought, caffeine was what she needed. She pushed off the chair and crossed to the coffeemaker. The scent of brewed coffee quickly enveloped the kitchen.

In her empty kitchen, with her troubled thoughts, Olivia sipped coffee and ate buttered toast.

The silence became heavy, and Olivia turned the television on for noise and turned it to the news. There was always something going on somewhere in the world. At that moment, the news report focused on the hashtag MeToo movement. The reporter went on to list the names of powerful men in politics, news media, and business who abused their position and sexually harassed women. Harvey Weinstein's name kept popping up.

Olivia winced at the idea of Harvey Weinstein exposing his fat, repulsive body as the women alleged he had. The image alone could leave anyone traumatized for life.

Ignoring the television, Olivia scanned the stove's clock. It was six a.m., and needing to fill her mind with something other than bad news and Bob for the next hour, Olivia muted the television and turned to her laptop. Clicking her book open, Olivia read the last chapter she wrote.

CATHERINE WAS AWAY FOR THE MORNING, and with the lack of inane conversation and gossip, the office was quiet and the staff productive. In the silence, you could hear the concerted industrious typing on laptop keyboards as emails were answered and purchase orders processed.

Productivity was the outcome of Catherine's absence.

Olivia checked her inbox and saw the emails from Vince and his team. The circle of love didn't work to Vince's satisfaction, and he resorted to celebrating his million-dollar sale in a group email to the entire company. There were thirty reply-all emails, and it was only ten o'clock in the morning.

The email from Vince went on to claim his million-dollar sale was a group effort, and he wanted to thank everyone for their support. To the savvy, Vince's email read as a feeble attempt to get his ego stroked. And he got it.

The email that followed seconds after from Sally read thank you, Vince, for your effort.

From Vince: Thanks, Sally.

From Sally: You're welcome. Keep up the excellent work.

From Jan: Congrats, Vince.

From Vince: Thank you, Jan.

From Michael: Way to go, Vince.

From Vince: I appreciate the email, Michael.

From Joshua: Keep it up, Vince.

From Vince: Smiley face.

From Elvira: Way to go, boss! A million dollars sale is very impressive.

From Vince: Thanks, Elvira. Winking emoji.

From Catherine: I'm very proud of our newly appointed Vice President.

From Vince: Thank you very much for your support, Catherine.

From Sally: Wow! Congratulations on your new title, Vince. I look forward to working with you and taking the company to the next level.

On and on it went. With a few clicks of her mouse, Olivia purged the emails and moved on to address the emails from her customers.

There was one from Gabe Green, and Olivia's spine instantly stiffened. Clicking it open, Olivia was pleased to see it was a purchase order for the product that only days ago he blasted her for shipping to the stores.

"Hey, Olivia." Vince sidled to her desk with a coffee cup in hand and that smirk she wished she could slap off his face. "I sent you an email to book a ten-minute meeting with you this morning."

It was probably in the batch she'd deleted. "Sorry, I haven't read all the emails."

"Do you have time now? Ten minutes, top."

Olivia shrugged. "Sure."

"I'm on my way to the kitchen to refresh my coffee. Can I get you one?" Vince smiled at her.

Her mouth in a stunned O, Olivia shook her head.

Bright sunlight pouring through the large picture window lit Vince's office. Framed prints of motivational quotes hung on the freshly steel-gray painted walls. One read, *Surround Yourself With People Who Are Going To Lift You Higher.* The other one said *Synergy Is What We At Sullivan Foods Strive For.*

The high gloss black lacquer desk was neatly organized. Angled at one corner of the desk, the laptop was opened to the email folder with fifty one-line emails of praise. Next to the laptop was a white leather penholder full of pens, and before Vince, a blank lined yellow pad was ready for him to pen the million-dollar ideas rolling in his head.

Vince closed the door, walked around the desk, and sat. His eyes on Olivia, he leaned back into the buttery soft leather of his chair. "Catherine told you she's promoted me to Vice President and that I'm to take over when she's not here."

"She mentioned something in passing." Olivia could see dust drifting like snowflakes floating around Vince in the sun's golden light.

"Catherine let the cat out of the bag in the email she sent me a few minutes ago, but an official announcement is being drafted and will be sent out this afternoon." Vince took a long sip of coffee and surveyed Olivia's face over the rim of his cup. "Are you all right, Olivia? If you don't mind me saying, you're looking worse for wear this morning."

Olivia didn't respond.

"If there's anything you'd like to talk about, I'm here for you. I believe in the open door policy style of management."

Olivia shot him a cagey stare out of her blue eyes. "I'll keep that in mind."

"Good." Vince's eyes shifted from Olivia's. "So, I wanted to talk to you about Gabe Greene's account."

She felt the tension ripple on her shoulders, down her spine to the flutter in her belly. "What about it?"

Vince straightened in his chair and poised himself tall. "I'll say this straight out. I'm taking the account and giving it to Elvira."

Olivia felt her lungs choke up. "What are you talking about?" This was only the beginning, she thought. Vince was poised to take everything from her. "It's my account, one I've worked on for years." Put up with degrading crap and verbal abuse that caused her an ulcer.

Vince held his hands up in the air, palms out. "Hear me out. You and Gabe are constantly butting heads, and I think Elvira is a good-looking woman who can keep him … engaged."

Did she hear right? He was pimping Elvira to boost his credibility.

"I thought you could take her out on your next visit to Gabe and introduce her."

Disbelieving, Olivia eyed Vince for a moment. "Let me get this straight. You're taking an account I've worked on for years to give to Elvira, who has all of a few months of experience, and you want me to make the introduction before she takes it over?" Olivia said, perplexed.

"Yes." Vince steepled his fingers and brought them to his chin.

Why me? Olivia asked herself.

She did everything right. She worked hard, stayed out of everyone's way. She was a good person—as much as she could be in a world stacked against her.

She had survived a bad marriage and financial ruin. She raised her thirteen-year-old sister when her father died. Olivia put Lottie through school and supported her until Lottie met Ken, an up-and-coming architect, in university.

Olivia did everything right. Why was the world against her?

Olivia looked from Vince to the framed words on the wall and back to Vince. "Does Catherine know about this?"

"She sanctioned it. It's for the benefit of the company, Oliva."

"Yes, I bet she did." Olivia froze Vince with her stare.

It was a matter of time until Vince took everything she had worked hard to achieve in the past twenty-five years and pushed her out.

Thrusting the door open, she stormed out of his office.

OLIVIA SAVED THE WORD DOCUMENT AND clicked it closed. It didn't sound perfect, and she still wasn't getting the ah-ha feeling, but it was her first draft. She hoped that she would get the feeling soon.

Olivia walked to the window and cast eyes to her backyard with the coffee cup in hand. Dawn had broken through the eastern sky, and the sun beamed brightly. There would be no rain this morning, as the weather channel forecasted. Meteorologists were the fortune tellers of the sky.

The air smelled of rich wet earth from last night's rain. Olivia watched two squirrels dart across the fence, and the neighbour's dog barked at them from behind the glass sliding door. In fifteen seconds, Brady went quiet. No doubt, Maryanne set Brady straight and silenced him.

Flashes of her and Bob sitting outside on the backyard patio on Muskoka chairs, sipping wine and talking, came to Olivia. It wasn't all bad with Bob, but it was short-lived.

They were young. Bob was an up-and-coming lawyer with a bright future. He stood to take over his father's law firm when he retired. Until then, Bob aimed to work on his law degree, followed by a master's degree. Upon graduation, Bob was to move into the corner office next to his father's to learn the intricacies of applying the law and managing the firm.

It was the criteria laid out by Bob's father for Bob to inherit the firm—or so Bob told Olivia. Olivia believed him. Robert Huntley Jr. was the son of Robert Jonathan Huntley Sr., a respected, renowned legal mind.

Although born into old money, Bob refused to live off his father's wealth. He wanted to make his own way and be his own man. An admirable trait in the man Olivia married.

Olivia's father thought so too, and to help Bob and Olivia save money to buy their future home, the newlyweds moved into the basement of her childhood home.

On their second anniversary, Olivia raised the idea of children to Bob. She was ready to start the family she had always wanted. Bob wasn't. He never intended to become a father. The notion of being a father and burdening himself with the responsibility of a child for life wasn't an appealing proposition.

It was the first time he'd said so to Olivia.

Olivia's attempt to change Bob's mind failed. Bob was adamant.

Disheartened by the notion of not being a mother, Olivia became withdrawn and depressed, and Bob turned to others to fulfill his sexual needs.

Bob's extracurricular activities came to roost when he infected Olivia with an STD. Suspicious of everything now, Olivia dug deeper into Bob's activities and what Olivia uncovered shocked her.

Bob never attended university, let alone attained his degree. Bob didn't intern at his father's firm. He never had. Where and how he spent his days was a mystery, although Olivia had her suspicions. Demanding answers, Olivia lobbed question after question at Bob.

The resentment bubbled up in Bob, hot and fierce at her interrogation. *He* was the man of the house. *He* set the rules, not the woman he married, to spite George, the man who thwarted his career by robbing him of the captain title of their high school football team.

Losing quarterback to George had grave consequences for Bob. It was the last straw for Robert James Huntley Sr. in a long line of disappointment Bob brought to his father.

Bob's drinking and the parade of women in his life was a boy's way of crossing into manhood, his father reasoned. Bad grades could be improved with tutors. A Huntley losing quarterback to a boy whose father was the school's custodian was unforgivable to Robert James Huntley Sr., who was MVP for four straight years. George attended the prestigious school only because his father was on their payroll, and his son was entitled to the privilege.

Bob's relationship with his father was tenuous before losing out to George. After his loss, his father practically disowned him. He cut off Bob's unfettered access to his trust fund and set him up on a meagre allowance—something Bob didn't know how to do. His BMW was replaced with a second-hand Ford, and credit cards were cancelled.

It felt like the apocalypse for Bob.

Bob aimed to break George as he broke him.

Stealing Olivia, the woman George loved, from under his nose was how Bob chose to break George—even if it meant jumping into marriage.

When Olivia confronted Bob about the STD and what she had uncovered, he became controlling and verbally abusive. Olivia's friends were unwelcomed, and working was out of the question. No good came from outside interference. Olivia was alienated from her friends, controlled, and left without money. Eventually, Olivia had no choice but to capitulate to Bob's coercion.

Bob hit the jackpot eight years into their marriage when Olivia's father turned the deed to the house to her and her sister weeks before his death.

Forging the paperwork to mortgage the home was simple. Presenting the documents to the bank on behalf of Olivia took some doing, but Bob was a resourceful man.

Bob went through two hundred thousand dollars in months and left Olivia to pay off the debt, or she and her sister would end up homeless.

Olivia's cell phone chimed, shattering her out of her reverie and dragging her back to the moment.

Tapping the alarm off, Olivia turned and filled Oreo's water and food bowl before she stalked upstairs to her bedroom.

Olivia was showered, dressed, and unprepared to face the day ahead by eight.

Chapter 13

OLIVIA FELT A quick twist the moment she pulled into the hospital's parking lot. She hated hospitals and hated the reason for being there more.

A long line of cars at the two entrance booths to the parking lot waited to claim an entry ticket. Foot traffic, some in hospital scrubs, and visitors made their way past the parking lot toward the hospital. An ambulance, red lights rotating and the siren wailing, pulled in front of the emergency entrance.

Olivia's phone shrilled. The caller was her lawyer, Amanda, returning her call. Thirty minutes later, they hung up. It turned out the only option to evade the possibility of absorbing any financial repercussions Bob may cast on her was to serve him with divorce papers—and soon.

Olivia needed time to think about that because how did you serve divorce papers to a dying man?

Olivia sighed under her breath.

She couldn't go back to a debt-filled life. She had neither the energy nor the tolerance to deal with the stress brought on by financial insecurity.

Her home, as small and dated as it was, was fully paid, and aside from the savings Olivia planned to live on for the next two years, she managed to put aside some money for retirement. Olivia was in no way a wealthy woman, but she had scrimped and saved for years to live a reasonable frugal lifestyle. Despite his impending death, Olivia wasn't amenable to giving that up.

Olivia remained in her car for the next ten minutes, her head resting on the steering wheel, and her tired mind floated.

Olivia understood the trials of life, but Christ, her trials were too many.

Her father emotionally and mentally left them when her mother, diagnosed with ALS, deteriorated, and it became too much for him to deal with. Olivia was a mere girl then. Still, she stepped in and did what had to be done.

Olivia became her mother's caretaker and parent to her younger sister.

Her mother suffered the ravages of the horrible disease for four years until a heart attack liberated her from the pain, suffering, and misery that had become her life. When she died, it broke her father, and he fell apart. Olivia became the adult at home and Lottie's sole parent. Olivia was seventeen and Lottie six, but she dealt with it all.

Olivia stepped into her mother's shoes and ensured Lottie focused on her studies. Olivia sacrificed her education to allow Lottie to pursue hers. Lottie would make something of herself. Lottie would be educated and become a self-sufficient, independent woman who would never need to rely on anyone but herself.

And Lottie did. Lottie got her architecture degree and met Adam, a fellow architect student with the same goals and dreams along the way. Lottie and Adam fell in love and married, and together they launched the successful L&A Architects. Lottie led the life Olivia never did, and Olivia couldn't be happier.

When Bob left Olivia, she alone dealt with the mess he left her. She wouldn't cast a dark shadow on Lottie's perfect life with her bad judgment. Alone, Olivia dealt with the heartbreak, betrayal, anger, and hate that churned in her for years after. Olivia did what she had to because it was either to swim or drown.

But Jesus, a person, could get tired of dealing, and Olivia was tired of dealing. Olivia sniffed back the tears and wiped her cheeks dry. She was a grown woman, not a child, and she wouldn't cry. Besides, crying resolved nothing.

The ringing cell phone had Olivia reaching for it. It was Lottie, and taking a deep calming breath, she answered it. "Hey," she said, sounding overly cheery to disguise her disenchantment.

"How are you doing?" Lottie said.

"Tired. I barely got a couple of hours of sleep last night." The sun was coming straight in at Olivia through the car's windshield, and she put down the sun visor.

The day was hot, sunny, and humid, but still. There was no wind.

"So, what's up with Bob?"

Olivia gave Lottie the Reader's Digest version of Bob's prognosis.

"Christ, Olivia, I'm sorry. But you don't have to take on this burden." Lottie's breaths came quick as she increased the speed on the treadmill halfway through the three-mile morning run she did every morning after dropping the girls off at school. Sometimes Lottie substituted doing laps in her indoor pool for running.

Most Days, Lottie was in her office, where she and Adam employed a staff of twenty, by nine or ten or eleven. She and Adam would be home by six to have dinner with the girls. Often there were black-tie galas or networking events that Lottie and Adam attended to schmooze their way into securing profitable contracts from the top builders in the country. Lottie led the ideal life Olivia wished for.

"I know, but I promised Cassie."

"Jesus, Olivia, only you would be agreeable to helping the blonde bimbo lover of the man who left you decades ago." Temper flared in Lottie's voice.

"It is what it is, and you shouldn't be so nasty."

"She is a blonde bimbo. You said so yourself." Lottie wound the treadmill down to walking speed to cool down.

"Well, yeah, but you shouldn't repeat it."

"Whatever. Anyway, it is what it is, is your answer to everything. If you can't tell the asshole you won't do this, I will."

"The man is dying, Lottie. He looks terrible." Olivia stepped out of the car, into the heat, and slung the cross-body bag on her shoulder. "He's in pain, lost his sight and...."

"Boo fucking hoo, Olivia. He deserves everything coming his way for picking up and leaving you overnight without a word. His suffering is payback. It's karma coming to claim the dues of his assholish behaviour."

"Jesus, Lottie." Olivia often envied Lottie's strength and eloquence, but now wasn't one of those times. "You wouldn't say that if you saw him."

"You're too soft, Olivia." Lottie drank water to hydrate. "I don't want to see you hurt again, but I know you, and you're going to see this through no matter what I say."

"I am. I...."

"Yes, I know. You need to do this," Lottie responded with a tone of resignation. "What about your writing? You said you're not feeling it, and this will certainly not help. Introducing this needless complication into your life will distress you and impact your writing."

Olivia's silence spoke volumes.

"Well, I'll be here when you need the pieces picked up, Olivia."

Olivia recognized pity when she heard it.

Chapter 14

THE HOSPITAL WAS thick with staff, medical personnel, and patients coming and going. At the bank of elevators, Olivia hopped on the first one to reach the ground floor and rode it to the fourth floor.

On her way to Bob's room, Olivia saw Cassie in the waiting room. Cassie wore the same faded jeans and brown sweater from last night and looked like she'd slept in them. Her hair, tied in a loose ponytail, underscored the swollen eyes red-rimmed from crying. Contemplatively she stared into the dark liquid in her coffee cup.

A tight, tense feeling gripped Olivia in the stomach. "What's happened, Cassie? What's wrong?"

Cassie's puffy, red eyes darted to Olivia arched in the doorway. "I was feeding him his breakfast. He eats so little now. He began to twitch, like really badly. Then he loses consciousness. The doctor's in with him has been for the past forty minutes."

Olivia sat next to Cassie and draped her arm around her shoulder. "I'm sorry, Cassie, you had to deal with that alone."

"The doctor said he had a grand mal something."

"A grand mal seizure?" Olivia fumbled in her handbag for a tissue and handed it to Cassie.

"Yeah, that's it." Cassie touched the tissue to her wet cheeks and eyes.

With measuring eyes, Olivia stared at Cassie. There was something else Cassie wanted to say but couldn't, and Olivia remained silent for a moment to give her the time she needed to gather her thoughts.

"The doctor says Bob has to go under pal...." She tapped her fingers to her head to summon the word. "Shit, pal, something care."

"Palliative care," Olivia said.

"Yeah, that's it. I sort of know what that means."

"It means...." Olivia stopped when she looked into Cassie's tired, sad eyes. "You don't need to worry about that right now."

"Bob's going to die, isn't he?" Their eyes met in a moment of understanding, and Cassie's tears came in sobs then. "God, he is."

Olivia heard the loss in Cassie's tone and saw the love in her eyes for Bob, as she had never felt for him or any man for too long. Olivia envied Cassie. She was twice Cassie's age and had never loved or cared for a man as deeply as Cassie did Bob.

"He's going to die, Olivia." Cassie's thin shoulders hunched.

Olivia considered telling her otherwise to ease her pain, but death was inevitable and lying would do her no favours. Olivia's hand closed over Cassie's and squeezed. "I'm afraid he is, Cassie."

"Oh, God." She gasped for breath.

"But you still have some time with him."

"You don't know that."

"I don't know how much time, but I plan to speak to the doctor to get some answers. I'll find out what I can."

"Okay."

"In the meantime, what do you say we plan a celebration of Bob's life? How does that sound?"

Cassie lifted watery eyes to Olivia. "Like a party?"

"Sure, it could be a party if you like."

"That sounds nice."

"Good, we'll start planning it right away." Olivia drew back and softly said, "I want to talk to the doctor. Will you be all right here?"

"No." Cassie mopped at the tears and wiped her damp hands on her jeans. "I'm coming with you."

IN BOB'S ROOM, THE NURSE IN blue scrubs and white running shoes stood on the right side of his bed, pressed buttons on the monitors and checked the IV drip. On the opposite side of the bed, the man in the white lab coat leaned over Bob and listened to his chest with his stethoscope. He moved the stethoscope's diaphragm around Bob's frail, pallid chest while he struggled for breath.

"Good to have you back, Bob. I suspect you had a minor stroke. I'll know more when Stephanie here arranges for the tests I've requested." The doctor slung the stethoscope around his neck.

"No tests," Bob's voice was a hoarse whisper.

"We need to do the tests to determine…."

"No tests. Useless." Bob's voice was weak but firm.

"All right, Bob. Steph and I will allow you to override us on this, aren't we, Steph?"

"Bob's our boss, Dr. Papa." Steph replaced the empty saline bag with a full one.

"It's agreed on. In the meantime, your lungs sound too congested for my liking and your heart's racing. I want to address both. No, Bob, I'm the boss on this decision." The doctor cut Bob off when he started to speak and rambled acronyms and unintelligible instructions to the nurse. "Steph is going to administer some great drugs to address both. You'll look after Bob, won't you, Steph?"

"Of course, I will, Dr. Papa," Stephanie replied with a comforting smile.

"Thanks, doc." Bob's voice was a whisper.

"Don't mention it. So, where's your sidekick? Did you finally talk her into going home to get some rest?"

"I'm right here, doc," Cassie said, and Dr. Papa turned to face Cassie, but his eyes stayed on the woman standing beside her. "This is Olivia, doc. She's a friend of Bob's and me."

Dr. Papa and Olivia's eyes met and locked. Olivia stood dazed, the shock registering on her face.

His short, cropped hair was dashingly grayed at the temples. His skin was dusky gold. His dark eyes were set too far apart above a nose too large for his oval face, but they exuded intelligence and wisdom. For a fifty-ish man, his medium-height frame was athletic and toned.

"Is he all right, doc? Is he okay?" Cassie rushed to Bob's side.

"Bob's going to be fine. Steph's going to administer some great drugs that will make him comfortable," Dr. Papa said, his eyes never leaving Olivia.

Olivia stared for a moment longer. When the shock receded some, with every appearance of calm, she said, "Hello, George."

"Hello, Livy."

"Livy? Do they know each other?" Cassie whispered to Bob, with STEPH curiously looking on.

Bob hushed her. "Give me a play-by-play of what goes on between them."

"It's been a long time," Olivia and Bob said in unison.

"It has." Olivia forced her feet to move and walked closer to him.

George could smell her perfume. She'd upgraded from the cheap lilac scent he remembered so well to Trésor. The long spill of chestnut hair tumbled around a face untouched by time. Her sapphire-blue eyes mesmerized him then as they had decades ago. She wore a salmon blouse and black pants over graceful curves that weren't there when he knew her all those years ago but looked good nonetheless.

Olivia offered her hand because she couldn't think of what protocol dictated in the situation.

George took her hand and held it tight. "Too long."

The connection unlocked long-stored memories, and they unspooled and flooded both like a classic black-and-white motion picture. She felt his thumb tracing the contours of her hand. Her breath hitched, her heart thumped, and she snatched her hand from his grip.

"You look great, Livy." Colour burned in Olivia's cheeks. George remembered how she blushed at compliments sent her way.

"Both you and I know that's a lie."

"You do, Livy. Have you ever known me to say something I don't mean?"

Olivia nervously tucked a strand of hair behind her ear. "You look better than great." She felt as if she'd stepped back into her awkward teen years.

A long silence lingered, and Cassie's brows furrowed as she watched the uncomfortable eye contact between Olivia and George. In the months Dr. Papa treated Bob, she'd never known him to be at a loss for words.

"Olivia, maybe you should ask Dr. Papa the questions about Bob you wanted answers to?" Cassie felt Bob's weak attempt to squeeze her hand to silence her.

"Yes, questions." Olivia searched her handbag for her notes. "I have several questions I want to ask you, George, ah, Dr. Papa."

"George, for an old friend is good enough." His eyes clung to her.

"Yes, well, ah, George. I've read up on Bob's condition on, umm, the Dr. Google." The white lab coat was more intimidating than George was unsettling. But then doctors always had that effect on Olivia. "I made notes of questions I'd like you to answer for Cassie and me."

"I'm happy to answer any questions you have. Why don't we step into my office? You don't mind staying with Bob, Cassie?"

"I want to hear what you have to say, Dr...." Cassie felt Bob's frail hand squeeze. "Sure, I'll stay with Bob."

"Okay. Let's head to my office, Olivia." George placed his hand on the curve of Olivia's back, and she made a noncommittal sound as he led her out of the room.

Chapter 15

GEORGE OPENED THE door of his office and stepped aside to allow Olivia entry. Bright beams of late morning sun leaked through the louvred blinds on the windows to light the room bright.

George removed the stethoscope around his neck and lab coat and hung both on the coat hanger by the door. He took a seat behind the ornately carved oak desk, and Olivia sat in the guest chair across from him.

The desk was neat and orderly. Patient files were neatly stacked on the sideboard behind him. Mount Sinai sew-sawed on the laptop screen sitting on the desk. Two Montblanc pens, a pad of yellow Post-it notes, and lined paper rested on the blotter before George.

His propensity for order endured.

George's diplomas and the many accolades earned over the years hung on the wall behind him. The bookcase was stacked with burgundy leather-bound medical books. It was a professional man's office, and George looked good in it.

"Would you like a cup of coffee?"

"Yes, I would." Olivia didn't, but she needed something to wet her dry mouth.

George crossed to the coffee maker on the sideboard and poured coffee into two white cups with the words Mount Sinai printed in bold red letters.

"You still take one cream and two sweeteners in your coffee, Livy?"

"Yes." He remembered. "No one's called me Livy in a long time."

George tore open two packets of sweetener, tapped the powder into the cup, and stirred. "I always liked the name, Livy. It suits you." He walked the coffee back to the desk and handed Olivia her cup. "Have Bob or Cassie told you everything?" He sat.

"I think so." Olivia lifted her coffee to her lips and drank. The coffee was surprisingly good.

"Glioblastoma multiforme is rare among all cancer types and occurs more often in older adults." George brought the cup to his lips.

"Bob's fifty-five. He's still young," Olivia said.

"Yes, he is, and if what you're saying is whether I'm certain of his diagnosis. I can assure you I am." George set the cup down on the blotter.

"I'm not questioning your competence, George."

"There's nothing wrong with questioning and opting for a second opinion. In cases like this, it's essential, and I encourage it. I consulted with three colleagues, and each concurred with my diagnosis. The disease is terminal, Olivia." George showed pure emotional kindness as he laid the facts for Olivia.

Understanding that what he'd just told her preyed on her mind and went deep enough to make her withdraw into her thoughts, George fell into the silence with her.

Olivia's face set in lines of worry. What did she do with information like that? Nothing George said was news to her, but it suddenly felt like an unmistakable moment of reality slapping her in the face. Her problems suddenly seemed so futile. Life was so fragile and fleeting.

Catherine, Vince, Gabe, and the stress they brought on seemed pointless, mindless, and senseless. Why did it take death to touch your life to realize it?

Olivia set her cup down on the coaster George set in before her. "How much time does he have?"

"Hard to tell. Maybe two, three months, possibly four. I'm sorry, Livy." Olivia said nothing, and George joined her. "Are you all right, Livy?"

Olivia looked George in the eyes. "I feel so helpless, George. What do I do with this information?"

"We ensure that his remaining days are pleasant and as comfortable as possible. I spoke to Cassie about hospice care. It's designed to provide the best quality of life for people near the end of life. They take care of his daily physical and emotional needs and monitor the cocktail of drugs that will ease his pain."

Olivia rose and walked to the window. "It doesn't seem right to leave a dying man under the care of strangers during the last days of his life, and I can't see Cassie allowing it."

"Yes, she's rather fond of him."

"Fond of him? She's completely and utterly in love with him." Olivia could almost feel the weight of George's look. "What?"

"The relationship between them is not what you think, Livy."

As much as the sound of him calling her Livy brought a smile to her face, Olivia gave him a hard look. "It doesn't matter what I think. I don't judge. It's their life."

He smiled. The fire he saw in her eyes was the Olivia he remembered. "Sounds to me as if you are judging, and it isn't what you think."

She looked directly into George's brandy-brown eyes. "I see Bob laid out his life's regrets and the sins of a dying man to you in search of absolution as well?"

"He did. He also knew I'd become a neurologist and searched me out to take him as a patient. He's told me a lot in the six months he's been my patient."

"Sounds as if you've forgiven him."

"It sounds as if you haven't."

"No, I haven't. Some things cannot be forgiven. Some words are impossible to forget. He ruined my life for purely selfish reasons. Forgiveness doesn't come as easily to me."

He gave her a critical scan. "Yet you're helping him nonetheless."

Agitated, Olivia paced. "How do you say no to a dying man? Besides, I doubt he told you everything."

In Olivia's defiant eyes, Bob saw the passionate Olivia he knew. "Why don't you tell me everything over lunch? We can discuss Bob's treatment, and you can tell me about your life." George held out a hand for hers.

The ring on his left hand was the second reality of the day to slap her in the face.

Chapter 16

OVER MORE WINE—to calm frayed nerves—than Osso Buco and risotto, Olivia told George what Bob did to her. She told him why he proposed marriage. "It was solely out of spite that he asked me to marry him." She polished off the wine in her glass.

"You accepted." George pointed out.

Olivia waved the waiter down and asked for another glass of red wine.

"Would you like one too, Dr. Papa?" The waiter, sharply dressed in a white shirt, bow tie, and black pleated pants, asked as he picked up Olivia's empty glass.

"Just for the lady, Jason, I'm on call. I will take a coffee refill." George took a bite of the buttered roll.

"Certainly, Dr. Papa. Coming right up, Dr. Papa."

Olivia said when they were alone again, "He's certainly enamoured with you."

George's mouth tipped up at one corner. "He's enamoured with his tip. I tip generously."

Now, her mouth tipped at one corner. "Since when?"

"Good to see you haven't lost that snarky wit," George added cream and sugar to his coffee.

That was the furthest thing from the truth. Olivia had lost everything she was. She'd lost her courage, her joy for life. Life sapped Olivia of the fearless woman who planned to conquer the world and scale mountains.

Responsibilities, financial obligations, and the wrong decisions made along the way tend to do that to a person.

"You should eat something, Livy. You've never been able to hold your wine on an empty stomach."

"Stop being a...."

"A doctor?" George finished and offered a dimpled grin.

Her eyebrows rose in mild disdain. Olivia picked up her wine glass and took an appreciative swallow.

"You like wine."

"I like its effects. Anyway, to clarify, I accepted Bob's proposal because you never said what I wanted to hear, and he did."

George stopped cutting into his Osso Buco and set the fork and knife down. "He didn't mean it, Olivia."

"Yeah, well, no, he didn't." She knocked more of her drink back.

"I couldn't say it because I'd mean it, Livy, and I couldn't follow through once I did."

Olivia drew a sharp breath through her nose, shook her head. "What does that even mean?"

George could see her temper hadn't lessened as she'd aged. "I didn't know you wanted to get married so young. You always said you wanted to pursue your education, your writing career before tying yourself down with a family."

"It's not how it worked out. Is it? Two years we were together, and you never told me you wanted to become a doctor," she said, looking at the table next to theirs when there was a rustle of movement.

The couple stood to vacate the table. The dapperly dressed middle-aged man reached into his jacket pocket for his money, dropped a few bills on the table, and then turned to help the elegant, blonde woman with her coat. Threading her hand through the crook of his elbow, they walked out of the restaurant together, smiling. She wondered what the experience felt like.

George set down his coffee cup and touched her hand. "I'm sorry I didn't, but I couldn't tell you I planned to attend medical school, Olivia."

His wedding ring flashed like a beacon in the night, and her gaze moved around the room, looking for somewhere else to settle. "You don't need to say anything else. I'm sorry I brought it up. What's done is done."

"No, Livy, you deserve an explanation." George went silent as the waiter approached the table to set the refill of wine before Olivia and top up his coffee. "Thank you, Jason."

"You're very welcome, Dr. Papa. Enjoy. Holler if you need anything else." The waiter flashed an all-teeth smile before he moved to the following table.

"I didn't tell you I wanted to become a doctor because I didn't want to lose you." George watched the quick confusion in her eyes.

"Stop, George." Olivia sank back into her chair.

"My parents didn't have the money to pay for university. You know my mother was a house cleaner and my father the custodian of our high school. They lived paycheque to paycheque, and I couldn't burden them with additional financial worry. That meant I would have to work to put myself through school. I planned to work full-time one year and return to school the next. It was going to take me twice the time to finish med school. If I told you I loved you, I couldn't promise marriage for years. I couldn't ask you to put your life on hold for me, Livy.

You deserved better." George's gaze met the glacier-blue eyes narrowed in on him.

"And no, Livy, we couldn't have made it work. I watched financial problems make my parents resentful, make them grow to hate one another, and ultimately drive them to divorce. It wasn't what I wanted for you. You had so much heartache and challenges in your life, and I wanted only happiness and love for you." His hand ran down the length of her hair. "I'm sorry it didn't turn out that way for you, Livy."

Emotions swam into her eyes. She reached for his hand and ran a finger over his wedding ring. "Has love and happiness filled your life, George?"

"As much as it could. I have two children, a boy and a girl, nineteen and twenty. Both aim to study medicine and lead their own lives. My wife was also a doctor, a pediatric oncologist. She's ... retired."

"Good, I'm happy for you, George. You deserve nothing less." Olivia picked up her drink and took a sizeable, numbing gulp.

That made George smile. Subtlety was never Olivia's strong trait. "You're quite the woman, Livy."

"How do you figure?"

"After all Bob did to you, and although you don't forgive him, you're willing to help him."

"It's not as noble as you think. I'm helping Cassie. She reminds me so much of me at her age, misguided, naive, and jumping head-on into a dumpster fire that will leave a dark mark inside her for life. She's too young to be dealing with all of it alone." Olivia huffed a frustrated breath. "It's so like Bob to put the burden of a dying man on a girl who's just starting her life. So, if I can help her, I will."

"She's not who you think she is, Livy."

"Really? Why would this young hatchling live with a man twice her age, care for him, be by his side, look at him with the doting eyes she does?"

"His daughter would."

Blue eyes popped wide, and her mouth opened in a stunned O. "Daughter? He never wanted children, Ever. Are you sure?"

George nodded.

Chapter 17

IN THE SULLIVAN Foods parking lot, Sondra sat with Olivia in her car. Lowered visors blocked the late afternoon sun. The windows were rolled up, and the air conditioner cranked up. Gordon Lightfoot's If You Could Read My Mind poured from the car's radio.

Still reeling from the bombshell George dropped on Olivia over lunch, she said nothing for some time, and Sondra joined in. The silence was as heavy as the dark cloud of grief hovering above Olivia, and Sondra gave her the time to gather herself.

For a long while, in silence, they ate Sondra's brownies and drank the coffee Olivia brought.

"You outdid yourself with this batch," Olivia said after some time.

"It's the real vanilla beans, compliments of Malcolm."

Silence.

"It's too much you're dealing with, Olive Oyl." Sondra split the brownie and gave Olivia one half.

"Life is unpredictable and random." Olivia absently took a bite of brownie and instinctively chased it with hot coffee.

"It is. Christ, I don't know what I'd do, how I'd react if I were told I had a few months left on this earth." Sondra tossed back a piece of brownie. "You need to walk away from this without remorse, Olive Oyl. It's already touching your life and just when you walked away from a stressful work atmosphere."

"Cassie is Bob's daughter, not his girlfriend, as I surmised," Olivia blurted out after a shared silence.

Sondra flinched as if he'd been stung. "Christ on a bike."

Olivia gave a quick bitter laugh. "Yes, the man who wanted nothing to do with children has a daughter." Yet another blow introduced to Olivia's system by Bob in the usual haphazard fashion.

Sondra glanced at Olivia. The hurt in her eyes only added to the pain Sondra felt for her friend. "I'm sorry, Olivia. I know you wanted children, but it could have been an accident. He did like dunking his doink."

"Yeah, I know." A small sigh escaped Olivia. "That's in the past. So, Malcolm graduated to the purchase foodstuffs phase. Have you assigned shelf and closet space at your place?"

Sondra gave Olivia a side-eye look and decided to entertain Olivia's comment because deviating from the painful topic was what her friend wanted and needed to do. With feigned keenness, Sondra entered the conversation. "Yes, our relationship has moved onto the purchasing foodstuff phase."

"That progressed quickly. So you will no longer refer to Malcolm as your coochie-sweet-spot-finder and call him your boyfriend. I will be a bridesmaid, won't I?"

"Of course, you will, babe. How do you look in a parka?"

"A parka?"

"Yes, a parka because I'll be getting married when hell freezes, and it will be so cold when it happens that you'll need one." Sondra rolled her eyes and hummed at her next bite of brownie. "Yeah, I don't think I can ever go back to using artificial vanilla again. I may have to put up with him moving in with me. You know how expensive that real vanilla shit is."

The smirk twisted Olivia's lips. "Christ, I can't believe Bob has a daughter." Olivia's mind seesawed between random thoughts.

"Yeah, I know."

"And from the expression on George's face, there's a story that needs telling. Unfortunately, he got paged by the hospital and left before he could tell it." Olivia watched Vince pull his new BMW SUV into the reserved parking spot. "His Lordship and his mistress are back."

"You mean sluttress."

Sondra and Olivia watched Elvira step out of Vince's SUV in a low V-neck shirt and tight white pants that left little to the imagination. Elvira brought a hand to her tousled hair to tame it in place while Vince smoothed and straightened his tie.

"Yeah, if those aren't the telltale signs of an afternoon delight, I don't know what is. What does that blonde Barbie see in that man-child?"

Olivia absently drank coffee. "My guess is she sees power and money."

It was a clear, sunny afternoon, with a taste of the incoming heatwave, and Sondra cranked up the car's AC.

"Power and money? Maybe someone should inform her we're a tiny company, not Amazon. I wonder how many brain cells they'd find if scientists dug beneath the blonde. Hey, how many blondes does it take to change a lightbulb?"

Olivia shrugged.

"None. They'd think it was night and sit in the dark waiting for morning to come."

There were some chuckles over that, and Sondra was happy to see Olivia smile.

"So this George Papa…." Sondra's voice lingered on the *a*.

"Papadopoulos." Olivia finished for Sondra. "It's a mouthful, I know, and it's why he goes by George Papa or just Dr. Papa."

"Just Dr. Papa. The man is a neurologist," Sondra spaced each syllable out. "And you didn't know it was him?"

Olivia read the message on her phone when it pinged. "It's Cassie reporting that Bob had the entire pudding cup."

"If I ever become sick and get to that stage, do me a favour and end it." Sondra sipped on coffee.

"No can do. Get lover boy to do it. And to answer your question, I didn't have a clue Dr. Papa was George until I met him. It never occurred to me Papa was short for Papadopoulos or that he'd be a neurologist. I'll tell you, he looks great. A Little older, a little grayer, but it gives him an air of sophistication."

Sondra looked surprised. "Do I detect lust in your voice Olive Oyl?" Olivia's cheeks took on a faint tint of pink. "Don't get all shy on me. This is a good thing. You're interested in this man, a man. I a time I wondered about you batting for the other team for a while, not that there's anything wrong with that. I'm tickled pink." Sondra giggled uncontrollably.

The effect of the brownie was taking effect, Olivia thought. "Don't think I wasn't tempted to switch teams for the more understanding sex. And even if I were interested in George, he's married."

Sondra embraced Olivia and held her tight. "I'm sorry, Olive Oyl. Even I don't cross the married line." The words tapered off to a spontaneous bout of laughter.

"I can't breathe, Sondra." Olivia attempted to free herself from Sondra's near stranglehold.

"Sorry, Olive Oyl." Sondra burst into giggles that went on for thirty seconds. Once she could compose herself, she reached for another piece of brownie, but Olivia took it from her.

"You've had enough."

"Yeah, maybe you're right." Sondra made a little snorting laugh. "Okay, okay, okay, back to George of the jungle, your high school sweetheart who's a gynecologist."

"A neurologist." Olivia dug out her cell phone and called Malcolm. "It's Olivia. ... Shut up and listen. ... Fine, I'm rude. Sondra is high as a kite. She's had one brownie too much. There's no way she can come back to the office. ... No, it's not my fault you introduced real vanilla beans to her. She can't seem to get enough of it. ... It is your fault. ... Shut up and listen. You need to tell them she's not coming back. ... I don't know. Make something up. I'm taking her to my house, and you can pick her up after work. ... Christ, Malcolm, we're not acquainted intimately enough for me to comment on whether she'll perform better when this high. My guess is she will," Olivia added after a short pause. "Anyway, get her handbag from her desk and bring it with you tonight." Olivia hung up before Malcolm could get the next word in and started the car.

"It would be way better if your doctor was a gynecologist." Sondra gave Olivia a wink.

Olivia rolled her eyes. "Buckle up."

Sondra let her head fall back on the headrest. "Just your luck to run into an old beau, and he happens to be married."

Olivia turned right onto Maple Road. "Yeah, the story of my life, but it was nice to see him again, and I am happy he's doing well. In my wildest dream, I never imagined he'd end up anywhere so austere. He's come a long way, considering his father was our high school custodian."

Understanding flashed in Sondra's blurred eyes. "So that's why you dumped his ass for Bob. My sweet, unassuming Olive Oyl, you're a snob."

Eyes, blazing with guilt and shame, stared straight ahead at the road coming at her. "That's part of it."

"Don't leave me hanging. What's the other part?" Sondra lowered the window halfway and breathed in the air that flowed in.

"He never told me he loved me, not once."

Sondra breathed in deeper. "And you fell for it when Bob did."

Olivia nodded. "I was nineteen. What do you expect?"

"Well, I hope you've learned it's better when those words come at a trotter's pace rather than stallion sprint."

"Has anyone told you, you become philosophical when you're high?" Olivia ignored the ping on her phone. "Anyway, a lesson hard learned, and now I've promised to take care of a man who told me he loved me to spite the man who's treating his illness and whom I was in love with every day. Irony has no boundaries."

"Now, who's the philosophical one? And was in love or still is?" Sondra watched Olivia's gaze focus on some distant point as she absently twisted the gold hoop in her ear. She'd leave the thought with her to figure out. "So, what have you decided to do with Bob?"

Olivia pulled into her driveway and killed the engine. "I've gone over all options, and I doubt Cassie...." Olivia stopped and breathed deeply, "Bob's daughter will be in favour of putting him into hospice. George doesn't think we can care for him at home. He says there are too much medication to manage and too much care for a fragile, dying, blind man. I will have to talk Cassie into admitting him into hospice. George can get a bed in one of the better hospices. It will cost out of pocket, but I have some money saved."

Sondra stared at Olivia quietly for a moment. "You're a saint, Olive Oyl."

"I gotta get inside the house to feed Oreo," Olivia said when she saw him at the window glaring at her with judgmental eyes.

Sondra opened the car door. "You need to fee me too. I'm starving."

Chapter 18

HAVING EATEN MOST of the large pizza and the chicken wings Olivia ordered, Sondra passed out on the couch with Oreo by her side. Both had a smile on their face and snored in concert.

It took some doing to persuade herself to make the call to Cassie, but Olivia gave in and placed the call. Cassie hadn't left the hospital since Bob was admitted and needed a good meal, a warm shower, and rest. In an hour, Cassie would make her way to Olivia's home to soak in the tub, eat the leftover pizza and wings, and get a good night's sleep.

Olivia took a quick shower to wash the miserable day off. In a fresh pair of jeans and a T-shirt, her wet hair bundled into a scrunchie, Olivia picked up her laptop and walked outside to the patio. The air was ripe with the fragrance pumping off her blooming garden. The grass had days of growth and needed to be mowed. It would have to wait another day or two.

Olivia sat on the Muskoka chair. Her legs stretched out, and her bare feet comfortably crossed at the ankles. Olivia opened the laptop and clicked her book open. She typed.

Casual Friday meant Jeans, T-shirts, and running shoes were the day's attire. Comfort was key. A warm sun filled the office with cheerful light. Yet, the tension in the room was as thick as condensed milk, thanks to Catherine and Vince, the doom and gloom whisperers.

Oliva reached for the cell phone when it pinged. It was Catherine texting again.

Where are you, Olivia? Call me. I need to speak to you. Urgent.

"I'm at my desk, Catherine," Olivia said loud enough for Catherine to hear. "I'll be there in a sec."

Olivia listened to the voicemail messages. The four messages were from Catherine. Deleting them, she eyed the unread emails on her laptop and saw Catherine asking where she was and to call ASAP. Olivia picked up a pen and the lined pad and psyched herself to face the unavoidable.

Catherine swivelled her chair to face Olivia and signalled her to sit in the guest chair. She wore a mauve silk blouse under a dark plum pantsuit with thin lapels. The diamonds at her ears, neck, and fingers twinkled under the sunlight shining through the window—Catherine's idea of dressing down.

Catherine leaned forward and rested her arms on the desk. "I've texted you a few times, called your cell phone, and emailed you."

"It's my goddamn lunch hour, Catherine. I'm entitled to eat a sandwich in peace," Olivia snapped with the ferocity to rock Catherine in her seat. At least, that was how it played in her head. "My cell phone battery died," she said politely and softly with a straight face. "What's so urgent?"

"You missed the last meeting, and I wanted to give you this." Catherine slid the book across her empty desk. "There's No I In Synergy is your next read. We'll be reviewing it at the end of next week."

Something, anything strike me down now, Olivia pleaded in her head. Olivia was never a fan of school homework, and adult homework was an even harder no.

"I have better things to do this weekend than read useless dribble, Catherine." If only Olivia could say the words in her head. The retorts came quickly, but it was futile when Olivia lacked the courage to tell them. "Great weekend reading material," Olivia remarked, fanning through the pages.

"It is. I particularly want you to focus on chapter ten, Cooperation, Collaboration, Communication, the three Cs of synergy."

"If Hitler had a copy of this book, we could have skirted two world wars."

Catherine gave Olivia an arched look. "I'd like you to read it and make notes to present during our meeting. Things like how you can improve personally and how to apply the three Cs to your workday and create teamwork. Like it or not, Olivia, I've entrusted Vince with the company's operation, and this type of positive reinforcement will be the norm."

"Good. Positive is good." Olivia welcomed a lightning strike straight to the brain then.

"Vince will be making changes to every department…." Catherine went on, and Olivia shut down when Catherine set off to spew the standard inane dribble and dug into her thoughts.

Of all the disappointments that touched her life, the defeated and trapped feeling she felt then was the most soul crushing. Olivia could pay her way out of financial ruin. She could forget the man who used and manipulated her but losing the job that gave her an identity undid all her hard work. It sapped her of the confidence she had worked hard and long to regain, but worse, it expunged her relevance. The essence of her professional life was who she was and whom Olivia identified with, and at this late stage of her life, relevance was all she had.

"Vince will be talking to you to go over the new rules," Catherine said.

Amid the debate with herself, Olivia said nothing.

If she stayed, the anger and the bitterness tightening her shoulder and stomach would consume her and resentment, anger, and hate would claw their way into her soul. She had been there years ago and had no interest in revising it.

"Are you listening, Olivia?"

Olivia wasn't, but she nodded her head. "Sure, whatever you want, Catherine," she said because saying otherwise would result in reliving the conversation, and losing another ten minutes of her life was unwarranted.

"It's that attitude you need to adjust, Olivia. You need to be respectful of Vince and his decisions. Vince's sole agenda is the company's betterment, whatever your feelings or thoughts."

Olivia rose to signify an end to the conversation. "I have a meeting to get to."

Catherine blinked her eyes wide in shock at Olivia's reaction. "If you don't wish to discuss this in more detail, then we're done here." Catherine watched Olivia quietly walk to the door. "You forgot the book."

Olivia rolled her eyes before turning to stare at Catherine, and Catherine thought she was searching for the words to refuse the book.

"Yes, thank you." Olivia walked back to the desk and picked up the book.

Could her life suck anymore?

Olivia edged toward the desk, took the book bound in canary-yellow with straw-coloured lettering and considered her choices. Stay with Sullivan, the company that was becoming a soul-crushing experience or walk out.

Vince was hell-bent on pushing her out of the company. Why Olivia was a threat to Vince was unclear, but she was, and her days at Sullivan's were numbered.

With frugal living, Olivia could live off her savings for a few years. But where would she turn on the third year when she ran out of money? What would she do when she ran out of money? Starting again at her age wasn't an option. Fifty-five may be the new forty, but that wasn't what her body and mind said. She was too tired and her spirit too broken to make a go of it again.

Why did life always have to come with strings?

After much consideration, Olivia decided to do the logical thing. Sometimes you have to accept your lot and move on.

Olivia read what she wrote. She wasn't feeling it. Why wasn't she feeling it? Everything she wrote was fact, real. Shaking her head, she saved the file and closed the laptop when the doorbell chimed.

Chapter 19

CASSIE ROUSED OLIVIA out of bed at seven in the morning. "We gotta go, Olivia. We gotta go now." She was hysterical, incomprehensible, and very loud and dragged Olivia to the surface of deep, exhausting sleep and roused Oreo out of his sleep. An unappreciative Oreo set off into a barking frenzy.

Olivia sat up in bed and wiped the sleep out of her eyes. "What's happened, Cassie? What's wrong, Cassie?"

"You need to drive me, Olivia. Now."

"Calm down, Cassie. Hush, Oreo, it's Cassie, our guest, remember." Olivia reminded Oreo when he continued to bark. After thoroughly studying Cassie with dark, piercing eyes, he settled back on the bed. "Now, where do we have to go, Cassie?" Olivia's eyed Cassie more closely now.

Cassie wore brown tights and a mustard hoodie. Her hair pulled back tight, set off Cassie's unpainted face, and Olivia saw what she hadn't before. Olivia saw Bob in Cassie's eyes, nose, and stride as she anxiously paced the room.

She debated whether Cassie, as Sondra said, was an accident or a planned baby. The only way Olivia would find out the truth was to ask Bob, and she wouldn't do so.

For one, the truth might hurt too much, and two, what's done can't be undone.

"I hope you don't mind. I borrowed some stuff I found in your laundry basket." Cassie's face was a little flushed.

"It's fine." Olivia sat on the edge of the bed and ran her hands over her face. "I'm sorry for staring. It's just that the outfit looks better on you than me," Olivia said truthfully.

Her life was a string of disappointments.

Olivia's reply caused Cassie to slam her brows together. "Sorry?" Cassie's voice stretched with the question. "Anyway, you need to drive me to the hospital now, Olivia." Cassie now looked as agitated as she sounded.

Olivia gave Cassie a pat of assurance. "Sit down and calm down. Now, tell me why we have to get to the hospital. Did Dr. Papa call you?" Olivia would have a word with George. She was Bob's wife, and he should be calling her with any issues instead of shocking Cassie.

"No, Dr. Papa didn't call. I just sorta sensed we need to get to the hospital."

Relief came in a wave, and Olivia walked to the bathroom and proceeded to brush her teeth and wash her face. "You sense things."

"Yes, I do. I can feel things." They were quiet for a moment. "You think I'm being silly."

Olivia poked her head out the bathroom door. "I don't, but Dr. Papa said he'd call us if anything changed, and he hasn't."

Cassie's eyes followed Olivia to the small closet. "But I felt it, Olivia, here." Cassie rested a hand on her stomach. "It woke me up."

"It's anxiety that woke you up, Cassie. You've been under a lot of stress for too long, and your thoughts are racing, and you can't switch off your brain." Olivia dug out jeans and a mustard-yellow T-shirt from her dresser. "So, next time, unless Dr. Papa calls, maybe don't shock me out of sleep on a feeling. Agreed?" She slipped on white running shoes, dropped her head forward, and finger-brushed her hair.

"Okay, sorry." Cassie sat at the edge of the bed, and Oreo rested his head on her thigh. "Aww, you are adorable." Cassie calmly stroked Oreo's head.

Oreo's inexplicable calming powers, Olivia thought. "Now, let's get breakfast. That sent Oreo racing out of the bedroom and down the stairs.

"I think he's hungry."

"What gives you that idea?" Olivia said, smiling back.

"Will we still go to the hospital?"

Olivia nodded. "After his majesty Oreo is fed and we have a good breakfast, we'll head to the hospital," Olivia said, deciding to push the conversation of hospice and Cassie's relationship to Bob for a later time.

Chapter 20

THE HOSPITAL CORRIDORS were alive with the chatter from nurses dispensing the morning medications to patients. Doctors made their rounds. Some patients pushed their IV poles as they took their morning stroll around the floor, while others rolled in their wheelchairs. Some moaned or groaned for attention. Many wore the blue hospital-issued gown and showed pale arms and faces and some shamelessly exposed droopy backsides.

The scent of coffee and fried eggs in the intensive care ward dwarfed the smell of despair.

At Bob's room, Cassie ran to his bedside. He looked pale, and his lips were chapped. He didn't look as if he had a good night. "Hey, Bob, I...." Cassie went silent when George held a finger up as he pressed the tip of his stethoscope to Bob's chest and listened.

"Breathe in, Bob, exhale." George shifted the stethoscope over Bob's chest and listened.

"Is everything all right, Dr. Papa?"

George covered Bob with the triple layers of bedsheets and elevated the bed to thirty degrees. "He's as good as can be expected."

"That means he's not worse, right?" Cassie set a second pillow behind Bob to help prop him up. "You're not worse, Bob."

"No, I'm not, honey," Bob said in a gravelly whisper before George spoke the truth.

"Yes, he's not worse, but Cassie, you must consider putting Bob into palliative care. He needs the care the medical personnel of palliative care provide patients in Bob's stage of illness."

Cassie shook her head. "I looked up what palliative care means on the internet. Bob's not going into palliative care. You're not. I won't allow it." She firmed her lips in determination.

All three turned when Olivia walked into the room.

Olivia didn't expect George to be there and recognized it as a bad sign. "Is Bob all right?"

"You're here, Olivia." Cassie ran to Olivia and threw her arms around her. Cassie looked as agitated as she'd sounded this morning. "I told you I sensed something wasn't right."

"What's wrong?" Olivia felt Cassie's hand grip hers tightly as she led her to Bob's bed.

"Go ahead. Tell her, Dr. Papa. Tell her what you want me to do." Before George could get a word in, Cassie said, "He says Bob has to go into this palliative care bull shit."

Olivia gave George an apologetic look and mouthed, "I'm sorry. I haven't talked to her yet."

"He wants to throw Bob out of the hospital." Cassie took Bob's frail, limp hand in hers. "I'm not going to let Dr. Papa move you." Cassie didn't mask the fact George rankled her.

Bob lifted tired eyes to Cassie. "Listen to me, Cassie." His voice was soft, feeble. "Remember the conversation we had."

Now the tears came. "No, I don't want to hear it."

"You or I can't change the trajectory of life. I wish I could for you, but we can't."

"Stop talking." Cassie's crying cut through the silence of the room.

"I wish I could be here to take care of you. I owe you that, but I can't, Cass." Bob gasped and sucked air into his lungs.

"He's come down with pneumonia," George whispered in Olivia's ear.

"My time is coming sooner than later, and just as well, Cass. I can't have you sacrificing your life to look after me. You should be dating and causing my hair to turn gray. Well, grayer. You should be experiencing everything a twenty-one-year-old does not take care of a dying man."

"You're not dying, and I don't mind looking after you. You're the only family I have, Bob. You're my daddy, and I've just found you."

"And you, Angel, are the best thing that's happened to me. You changed my life, Cass, and made me see what I couldn't in so long." Bob struggled for air. "You're wonderful and you make me wonderful."

"See, you're a new person. You can't leave." Cassie swiped at the tears running down her cheeks. "You can't leave me, Daddy. Not you too."

"I don't want to, but I need to, Cass. I'm tired. My body's tired, and I need to rest. Can you understand that?"

Cassie inclined her head and remained silent.

"You will always be my angel. You will always be in my heart, and I'll always look up to you from where I'm going."

Cassie gave him a watery smile. "You always said it's more fun down there than up there."

"I love you, Cass." Love, true and profound, Olivia thought Bob incapable of, radiated from his eyes. Grief looked different on everyone, and on Bob, it looked atypical but good.

"I love you, Daddy." Tears were running down Cassie's cheeks unchecked.

A memory of another time came to Olivia. Bob and Cassie's conversation took her back to her mother's last day and the words she said to her and Lottie. The tears stung the back of Olivia's eyes at the memory.

In a moment of sheer weakness, Olivia stepped close to Cassie and wrapped an arm around her hunched shoulders. "We're going to take care of Bob, Cassie." George opened his mouth to say something, but Olivia held up her hand to silence him. "I'm bringing Bob home with me, George. Will you make that happen? Cassie and I will look after him."

Chapter 21

"YOU'RE BLOWING BEAUCOUP smoke up my ass," said Sondra when Olivia told her she couldn't talk on the telephone because she needed to sort the living room for Bob's arrival that evening.

"Are you high on your friend's brownies?" Lottie responded when Olivia told her of her plan to bring Bob home and house Cassie in the spare bedroom.

Hanging up on Olivia, Lottie threw on white leggings and a pale raspberry tank top and went for a run to clear her head.

Her sister was too much of a pushover, Lottie thought, picking up her jogging pace to a quick sprint. What Bob did to Olivia was deplorable and inexcusable, and he didn't deserve Olivia's empathy—even if he was on his deathbed.

Lottie's anger sprang from the guilt she had carried all these years for not seeing the bigger truth sooner.

Eighteen, when Bob left Olivia, Lottie was filled with teen angst to see beyond her needs and was blinded to Olivia's pain. Lottie didn't offer the support her big sister needed from the only family she had. Instead, Lottie fought and resented Olivia for stepping into her mother's shoes. Who was Olivia to tell her what to do?

Even with everything Olivia was working through, she put Lottie through university to realize her dream of becoming an architect and build a network of what she called "like-minded" friends. Because of Olivia's perseverance, Lottie went to school, got a master's degree, and met Adam, a "like-minded" architect who became her husband along the way.

Lottie's company, the career she carved out, and the man she married were due to Olivia's support and encouragement. Everything Lottie was and had was because of Olivia, who had worked her fingers to the bone to support her dream.

And not once had Olivia asked for repayment, but today Lottie would repay her big sister by looking after her.

Lottie turned left on Maple. Before she knew it, she was standing in front of Olivia's home and knocking on her front door.

"What are you doing here, Lottie? Shouldn't you be at work?" Olivia said when she opened the front door.

Lottie's face was wind-reddened, and her hair and face were damp with sweat. "Hello to you too, sis and to you, Oreo." Lottie bent down, framed his face with her hands and booped noses when he barked his welcome at Auntie Lottie. "I was working from home when I got your disturbing phone call. Are you going to let me in?"

Olivia stepped to the side, and Lottie walked in.

"I've come on a mission to bring logic to your mommy who's lost her mind," Lottie said, and Oreo barked.

"You wasted a run. My mind is set. I'm doing this."

Lottie slanted a look over her shoulder and gave Olivia a we'll-see-about-that look. "I need to hydrate."

"There's ice tea and homemade lemonade in the refrigerator."

"Water will do." Lottie walked to the kitchen, and Oreo went along, hoping for a treat. Untie Lottie was generous with the treats.

Lottie drank a tall glass of water and, to Oreo's delight, tossed him an oatmeal cookie from the cookie jar on the counter. Afterward, she and Oreo joined Olivia in the living room.

"What's going on here?" Lottie eyed the boxes.

"I need to make room for the hospital bed and the medical equipment they're dropping off in an hour."

"Hmmm, is Bob paying for all this?" Lottie said.

Olivia proceeded to wrap the porcelain figurines in newspaper. "Although I don't see how that's any of your business, Bob's doctor helped secure the medical bed and the equipment Bob required. He's also arranged for a nurse to visit Bob daily to administer the meds and offered home visits to check on him. We can take care of Bob between Cassie, the nurse, and me."

Her sister, the martyr, Lottie thought. "But why would you? And when will you find time to work on your book with all this going on in your life?" Lottie took the vases Olivia handed her, wrapped them in newspaper, and packed them in the box while Oreo barked at Lottie for attention.

"Stop getting into Auntie Lottie's way, Oreo." Olivia handed him his stuffed toy. "Go play with it in your bed." Olivia swivelled to Lottie when Oreo walked away with the gray whale in his mouth. "I have to do this, Lottie, and as for the book, I'll find the time."

"No, you won't or have you forgotten what it was like caring for Mom? It was time-consuming and draining. You were young then and had the energy. You're not so young anymore, Olivia."

"Well, thank you for the reminder. Help me push the couch to the window wall. The hospital bed's going in its place." Olivia flicked her eyes to the digital display on the PVR; it flashed 3:00. "I hope the bed people get here soon. The ambulance is due at five."

"So, when are you planning to sleep?" Lottie's voice was an inflection, but Olivia didn't hear it.

"What?" Olivia straightened the cushions on the couch.

"Between caring for Bob and this Cassie girl and working on your book, when will you have time for sleep or yourself?" Lottie fell back on the couch and tucked one leg under the other.

Oreo jumped on the couch and rested his head on Lottie's thigh.

"It'll be tough, but it won't be for long." Olivia fell limply on the couch. "Bob has only a few weeks left."

Disdain drained, and guilt flared. "I'm sorry, I wasn't thinking, Olivia."

"Don't worry about it. Bob and his daughter shared a tender moment at the hospital where he said goodbye to her and…." Olivia stopped for a moment.

The sad look on Olivia's face conjured up the memory in Lottie. "It took you back to Mom's last moments with us and what she said before she died."

Olivia nodded. "I remembered the sense of helplessness, emptiness, and the void I felt. It broke me, Lottie. I couldn't let Cassie go through it alone, just as I couldn't let you feel alone when you were hurting so much during Mom's last days."

Olivia's words hung heavy in the air, and they sat in silence for a few moments, lost in their thoughts.

"Well, if you need a helping hand, money, anything, don't hesitate to ask. I mean it, Lottie."

Olivia looked across at Lottie and closed a hand over hers. "Thanks, I know you do, but Bob's my responsibility. I'll deal with it." Olivia surged to her feet. "Help me finish clearing up the living room."

Olivia's cell phone pinged. She read the text from Catherine.

"Six months on, and she's still texting me by mistake." Olivia held the cell phone up for Lottie to read.

Reminder of tomorrow's team building meeting. Please don't forget to read your assignment.

"She gives homework?" Lottie picked up the box and followed Olivia to the dining room. "I'd have a mutiny on my hands if I ever assigned homework to my staff. They have better things to spend their time on."

"She assigns idiotic reading material, which is supposed to set the staff on a carpet magic ride to synergy land."

"Guess she's in the dark about your friend's brownies. That would set her off into a nice magic ride."

"Set the box down here," Olivia said, telling Lottie when Sondra offered Catherine a piece. "She's eating a brownie in front of the woman as she holds the square out in offer."

"Testicles of steel that girl has."

"Titanium is more like it." Olivia walked back to the living room and picked up another box to cart to the dining room. "I didn't think I had so much stuff. You can set that box down over there."

Lottie set the last box down in the corner. "So, where's Bob's daughter?"

"She's at the hospital. She's going to accompany him on the ambulance ride here. She's very attached to him."

"What's she like? Tell all." Lottie made a rolling hand gesture.

"She's twenty-one and very pretty. She must look more like her mother because I couldn't make the familial connection with Bob as easily. She seems like a nice girl."

"She seems like a nice girl? You're inviting this girl into your home and what you know about her is a half-ass observation."

Olivia stopped mopping the floor and gnawed on her bottom lip. "I haven't had the chance for an extensive conversation." She saw Lottie's brow wing high. "We've had bigger issues to deal with."

Her sister, the world's mother, Lottie thought. The word no wasn't in her vocabulary. "So, what's going to happen with the girl when Bob's gone?"

Olivia turned to Lottie and said in a low contemplative voice. "I don't know. I haven't thought that far ahead."

"Maybe you should. You may end up raising a teenager. I'll get that," Lottie said when the dryer buzzard sounded.

Olivia nibbled pensively on her lower lip as Lottie walked past her and out of the room.

Chapter 22

LOTTIE REACHED FOR the steaming cup of coffee and sipped. "I don't mind staying. I've had my assistant push my appointments to tomorrow, and Adam will finish the Robinson's drawings. I'm not going anywhere. I'm here to support you."

The kitchen was filled with the scent of freshly brewed coffee and chicken soup bubbling on the stove. Olivia, like their mother, believed chicken soup was the great balm for everything.

"Or is it more that you need to give everyone an eye over?" Olivia set cream and sugar on the table.

Lottie opened the door to the backyard when Oreo barked his command for his human to let him out. Lottie watched him dash to the maple tree and raise a leg. "That too, but only because I have this sister who's too trusting of everyone, and she needs a cynic like me to present an objective opinion." Lottie turned from the door and looked around the renovated kitchen.

The kitchen was small but, under her expert design, had become contemporary and functional. If only she could talk Olivia into modernizing the rest of the house, it would double its value and become a comfortable oasis.

"To present an objective opinion or judge?" Olivia said.

Lottie answered that with arched brows.

"Either way, I'm glad you're here. There's something else I haven't…." Olivia stopped mid-sentence when the doorbell chimed.

"Ignore it." Lottie clamped a hand on Olivia's arm when she got to her feet. "Finish your thought, Olivia."

"Later. I have to get the door. It's probably the people delivering the bed and the equipment."

The bed and equipment were set up just in time because, half an hour later, the ambulance pulled into Olivia's driveway. Nosy neighbours walking their dogs, gardening, or sitting on their porch enjoying the summer heat stopped what they were doing and flicked their eyes toward Olivia's house.

From Olivia's porch, Lottie watched Cassie exit the ambulance. She wore a lilac T-shirt and jeans with tears at the knees. Her blond hair was tied with an elastic band, and loose tendrils tumbled around her pale face.

Slinging the backpack over her right shoulder, Cassie led the paramedics rolling the stretcher past the short walkway lined with a purple wave of petunias.

"Hi." Cassie climbed the three steps and leaned in to hug Olivia. Dark shadows and fatigue dogged her moss-green eyes. "Thank you so much for doing this, Olivia, for everything." Her voice sounded tired, drained.

"Nothing to thank me for." Olivia slung an arm around Cassie's thin shoulders. "This is my sister Charlotte, Lottie, for short. Lottie, Cassie."

"Mine is Cassandra, like my mom's. Cassie for short."

"Hi." Lottie offered her hand, and Cassie took it. "I'm sorry we're meeting under these circumstances."

"Yeah, well." Cassie looked over at the man on the stretcher, and Lottie followed her eyes. "I guess you know, Dad."

Nothing could have prepared Lottie for what she saw. Lottie didn't recognize the man under the layers of heavy covers. His eyes were closed, sunken into their sockets, and his skin was sallow, almost paper-thin. For a moment, Lottie thought Bob wasn't breathing.

Out of regard for Cassie, Lottie bit back the choked gasp wanting to rise into a shriek. The hate and resentment, the bitterness eating at her for decades, dissolved into a melting pot of pure sympathy. No one deserved to exit this earth in this way, Lottie thought.

"Go to the living room, gentlemen, through the door and the first door on the right. The bed and medical equipment are set up there." Reaching for Cassie's hand, Olivia led her past the hallway to the living room.

"Let's get you something to eat while they get Bob settled," Olivia said to Cassie.

"I'm not hungry." Cassie dropped her backpack on the couch and unzipped it. "Dad's medications are all in here. I was hoping you could help me give them to him, Olivia. There's a lot of them."

"I will, but right now, we're going to get out of the way so the paramedics can get Bob settled, and you're going to get some chicken soup in you. Call us when you're done, guys."

"Will do, ma'am."

Olivia walked Cassie to the kitchen, where Lottie ladled soup into three bowls and Oreo ran from the backyard when he sensed visitors.

Cassie flashed a dimpled smile the moment she saw Oreo. "Hello." Cassie knelt, and Oreo raced toward her, his tongue lolling and a smile on his face.

"That's Oreo. He loves attention and loves to give it," Lottie said, "and he's spoiled rotten."

"We've met. Haven't we, boy?" Oreo gave Cassie a doggie grin.

"Soups on." Lottie set the bowls on the table.

Olivia reached into the cutlery drawer for three spoons. "How's Bob doing today, Cassie?"

"Not well." Cassie patted Oreo on the head before she stood. "He didn't sleep much last night."

Olivia set the spoons and napkins beside each bowl. "And from the looks of you, you didn't either."

Cassie shook her head.

"I set you up in the guest room. You can have a lie down after you eat. I'll watch over Bob."

Cassie started to say something, but Lottie held a hand up to stop her. "I'd do as she says. You don't, and there's no shutting her up. I know. I'm her younger sister and almost deaf," Lottie signalled Cassie to the chair.

"All right, I will." Cassie slid into the chair with a mirroring smile, and Oreo spread out at her feet. "Can I take a shower first?"

"Of course, you can. Consider this your home. After you finish your soup, Lottie will show you around and get you set up."

"I think he's hungry," Cassie said when she spooned soup, and Oreo rose on his hind legs and planted his paws on her thighs.

"He's always hungry. The dog can eat twenty-four-seven and never gain an ounce. He's the envy of every bitch he knows," Lottie said, making Cassie smile for the third time in minutes. "Get down, Oreo, and go play with your stuffed toy."

After her first taste of soup, Cassie spooned faster. "This is good. It tastes like my mom's."

The comment made Olivia and Lottie stop what they were doing and turn to Cassie, hoping she'd share more information.

Cassie didn't. She brought the bowl to her lips and slurped the remains of the soup. "Sorry, that was rude, but I haven't eaten in a while," she said when she felt Oliva's and Lottie's eyes on her.

"Can I get you a second bowl, or I can make you a sandwich," Olivia offered.

"A sandwich sounds good, and maybe another bowl of soup," Cassie added shyly.

"You get the soup, Olivia. I'll make the sandwich. I didn't see you bring any luggage with you. Ham and cheese with the works good for you?"

"Sure. I have a carry-on in the ambulance. Adrian, the paramedic, said he'd bring it in for me. Everyone's been so nice."

Lottie walked to the pantry and fished for the loaf of bread. Lottie reached for the ham, cheese, mayonnaise, lettuce, and tomato in the refrigerator. "Toasted or untoasted."

"Toasted, thanks. Dad says he wants to pay for all the expenses you're incurring. I have an envelope with two-hundred dollars in my backpack. It's all I…."

"Don't worry about that. Don't worry about anything. We have it covered." Lottie dropped the bread in the toaster.

Olivia's brows pressing together in puzzlement, she stopped the soup ladle mid-pour. "We?"

"Yes, we. I'm also going to help with taking care of Bob." Lottie reached for the popped toast in the toaster.

Olivia's eyes filled with disbelief, as Cassie's drenched in appreciation. "I, ah, I don't know how to thank the both of you." Oreo barked twice. "You too, Oreo."

"Pay it forward is all Olivia and I ask. You know, do a kindness to someone in need when the opportunity arises and so on. It's the kind of world I want my girls to grow up in."

"That sounds like a great world. You can count on me to pay it forward when I can. How old are your girls?" Cassie filled her mouth with the sandwich and left traces of mayonnaise around her mouth.

"Juliette is thirteen going on twenty, and Lexi...."

Lips ripe with a smile, Olivia left Lottie and Cassie talking to check on the paramedic's progress. She'd never been more proud of her sister.

Chapter 23

DESPITE THE SUNNINESS of the late afternoon, it was hard to smile. The weight of the day was on Olivia's shoulders. Bob woke up nauseous and confused. At one point, he lost perception and didn't know where he was or how he got there. It took some time to calm him down.

Bob couldn't keep food down. He hadn't been capable of drinking any of the broth she fed him. Olivia was glad for the IV drip the paramedics set up and the only thing hydrating Bob.

Everything inside Olivia shrank. She thought she'd left the emotional turmoil, the haze in her head, and the helpless feeling behind when she buried her mother and father.

"Bob's finally asleep. Who knows for how long? You should go home, Lottie. It's four, and the girls are probably home from school." Olivia sat in the red Muskoka chair on the patio next to Lottie.

The air smelled of cut grass and heat. Above them, birds flitted and chirped in song. Bees buzzed from bloom to bloom in the garden while cicadas sang their mating song.

"The girls are home. Mother and father-in-law are with them. She'll make them dinner, and he'll keep them entertained until Adam gets home." Lottie took a gulp of wine. "Cassie is still passed out upstairs, dead to the world."

"I don't think she has slept well in days." Olivia spun the stem of the wineglass slowly between her fingers.

"I think we have Oreo to thank for that. Snuggled close to her in bed, he helped her fall asleep."

Olivia's cell phone pinged. She read the text.

"It's Sondra checking in to see how I'm doing." Olivia texted Sondra that she was okay and Lottie was with her.

"She's a good friend, a nutty, high one, but a good friend nonetheless." Lottie paused, then said swiftly, "You're a good person too, Olivia. What you're doing for Bob and Cassie is admirable, but then she grows on you. She's genuine and affable and…."

"Lost and overwhelmed," said Olivia.

"Yeah, but if I know you, you will help her with that." Lottie's eyes followed the flight of two robins from the maple to the elm tree and disappeared in the tree's thick foliage.

"I have to." Olivia stared into her glass quietly for a moment. "She has no one else."

"What about Bob's family?"

"His parents died a few years back, and he and his sister aren't talking."

"Bob, the destroyer of people and relationships. I'm surprised he didn't send Cassie packing when she appeared in his life." Lottie picked up the bottle of Riesling and refreshed her glass.

"I'm sure there's a story there. As with any story, in time, it will be told." Olivia refused the refill of wine.

Lottie set the bottle down on the table between them. "Cassie's so young to be dealing with this alone. At least we had each other when Mama got sick."

"I know." Olivia stopped short to listen to the baby monitor on the table when she thought she heard Bob stir. "He's wheezing, struggling for air."

"You know this is a twenty-four-seven job."

"I know."

"You can't take care of Bob on your own. I'll help you as much as possible, but I have the girls, work, and Adam."

"I know, and I appreciate your offer to help, but I'll manage." Olivia set her wine glass on the arm of the chair and left her fingers on the stem to run up and down.

"You're not in your twenties like when Mom got sick, Olivia."

"Thank you, I'm aware of that, Lottie."

"Just saying." After a moment, Lottie said, "I have a customer who owns a nursing service. They offer at-home nursing care."

"Sounds expensive."

"I told you and Cassie I'd help, and I will." Lottie looked down at her cell phone and read Adam's text.

Leaving the office for home. Can pick u up on the way.

Lottie texted back. *Sounds good. See you then.*

"Adam will pick me up shortly."

Olivia sipped on her wine. "Not that I'm not grateful, but why are you being so helpful with Bob? You loathe him."

"So do you."

"I do, I did." Olivia corrected. "The bottom line is, right or wrong, I married him and like it or not, I feel he's my responsibility, not Cassie's."

That wasn't it, or at least not the whole story, Lottie thought. Her sister was the worst liar. Eyes cut away, shoulders hunched, were trademark signs Olivia was holding something back.

Lottie sipped thoughtfully, looking for the right words. "We went through this with Mom and know how difficult it is to deal with sickness and impending death. As much as I understood it wasn't Mom's fault, you become resentful, angry at the world, and jaded at that young age. So jaded. I wouldn't want that for the girls, and I don't want it for Cassie. She's young, impressionable, and doesn't look like she's had an easy life. This is adding to her struggle."

"Possibly, but either you or I know her well."

"We do, Olivia. She's us. When we were taking care of Mom, I wished and prayed that there was someone like the us we are now. Today's us can help that girl and should because when gratuitous, painful death gets its claws in you, it doesn't let go. It affects you and stays inside you," Lottie pressed a finger to her chest, "forever."

Olivia nodded. "Yes, it does."

"Good, then I'll call my customer and get a nurse in here immediately." Lottie's cell dinged. "Adam's here."

Olivia walked Lottie to the front door. On the way, they stopped to check on Bob. His breathing was shallow, barely audible, but he was asleep—or so the heart monitor indicated with its beeps.

"As much of an asshole as Bob is, he doesn't deserve this," Lottie said.

"I'm just worried now where Cassie will end up after Bob's gone."

"I'm sorry you're dealing with this, Olivia," Lottie said when Olivia went contemplative. "But you're not alone. I'll be here with you. I hope it doesn't stop you from writing your book."

"Let's not have this conversation now, Lottie," Olivia replied with a sigh. Talking about her writing venture would have Olivia spilling that the book wasn't coming together as she hoped and lead into a conversation Olivia had no interest in pursuing then.

"Fine," Lottie said, but only because she heard the day's fatigue in Olivia's voice.

"Come on, let's not keep Adam waiting." Olivia opened the front door and saw Adam and George on the porch introducing one another.

"Hey, Olivia." Adam moved to give Olivia a brotherly hug before he turned to kiss Lottie on the cheek. "This is Dr. Papa, Bob's oncologist. This is my wife…."

"Hello, Lottie," George said before Adam could finish.

"You're Bob's doctor?" Lottie's voice hitched one octave. "Christ, small world." Lottie gave Olivia a long, inquisitorial stare.

Now, Adam looked confused. "You know each other?"

"We do, from way back." Lottie eyeballed George. "You cleaned up well, George."

Solemn dark eyes and gray traces in his short, neatly combed hair gave him an air of authority. His face, stubbled with the day's growth, looked good on the olive face. He wore a blue silk tie against a white shirt and chocolate-brown pleated pants. He was never one for flair, but things changed, Lottie thought.

In George's right hand, he carried a black medical bag. George Papadopoulos, the school nerd, a neurologist. Things did change.

George's lips curved into a smile. "Thanks. You, too, cleaned up nicely, Lottie."

"You'd think my sister would have mentioned you." Lottie cocked a brow at Olivia.

"I started to tell you earlier," Olivia said.

"Well, whatever this is, you'll tell me in the car because we have to get home." Adam reached for Lottie's hand and pulled her away when she didn't budge.

"I want every sordid detail," Lottie called over her shoulder.

Chapter 24

GEORGE WAVED AT Lottie, eyeing him sharply out of the passenger car window as Adam rolled the BMW out of the driveway and drove off. "She hasn't changed."

"Not one iota, but it's a good thing. She's an architect. She and Adam run a successful firm, L&A Architects. You know them?" Olivia asked when his brows shot up.

"Of them. Her firm is working on the design for the new hospital wing. Bunny and Taylor Robinson donated twenty million dollars and commissioned L&A Architects to do the design."

"Yes, she mentioned something about that in passing. I didn't know it was your hospital." Olivia led George into the house. The familiar scent of chicken soup, a smell George distinctly remembered from his visits to the house, painted the air.

Not much had changed in the home he and Olivia had spent nights studying or watching television or doing what young teenagers in love do.

The narrow entry hallway was as he remembered and as unpretentious as its owner. The parquet floor was polished to a shine, and the walls had a new paint job, but the same square, floral light fixture hung from a white popcorn-covered ceiling. It was a small home full of memories, a love letter to the past.

Oreo sniffed out company, jumped from the bed where he and Cassie lay, and came running down the stairs to greet the visitor. With a couple of barks, he introduced himself.

"And who's this little fellow?" George scratched Oreo's head.

"That's Oreo, down boy." Cassie walked down the stairs. She looked happier than he'd seen in a while. She wore stonewashed denim shorts and a white shirt, and her straight hair fountained around her face to her shoulders.

"Hello, Cassie." George wrapped her in a hug when she threw her arms around him. "You look well."

"I've eaten and showered, if that's what you mean."

A wide smile settled on George's face. "I meant rested, but that's good too."

Cassie picked Oreo up when he wouldn't stop barking. "Shh, Oreo, this is Dr. Papa. He's looking after Daddy. He doesn't like it when I don't introduce visitors to him. Give Dr. Papa your paw."

Smiling warmly, George reached to shake the offered paw. "It's a pleasure to meet you, Oreo. Now, if you'll excuse me. I need a few minutes with Bob," he said to Oreo, who lapped his muzzle.

"He's in the living room. You know the way. Have you had dinner? I have chicken soup," said Olivia.

"How can I say no to the famous Falco chicken soup? But it'll have to be a quick bowl. I need to get home."

"Yes, of course." Olivia masked her disappointment. "When you're done with Bob, meet me in the kitchen." Olivia turned to head in that direction.

"He likes you, really likes you, Olivia," Cassie said, watching Olivia light the fire on the stove.

"George is a friend." Olivia ladled soup from the larger pot into a smaller one and set it on the burner to heat. "We knew each other in our teen years and then lost track of one another."

"I know. It was because of Dad." Cassie met Olivia's eyes and exchanged a moment of complete understanding. "But now you've come together again. Maybe you can become more than friends."

The comment caught Olivia by surprise, and she turned to face Cassie. "Why would you say that?"

"Sorry, am I interrupting something?" George stopped in the doorway when he sensed he'd walked into something he shouldn't inject himself into.

"Nope, have a seat, Dr. Papa. How's Daddy doing?"

"As well as can be expected. The antibiotic seems to be doing the job, and his pneumonia is improving. He's resting right now."

"Good. Come on, Oreo. Let's go upstairs. I'll take the baby monitor with me so you can have a nice visit." Cassie ran out of the kitchen before Olivia could say anything, and Oreo followed.

"She certainly seems cheerier."

"Yes. You can thank Oreo for that. They've become inseparable." Olivia transferred the bubbling soup from the pot to the bowl and set it on the table before George.

"I'm glad. She deserves happiness in her life. The last year has been difficult on Cassie." George scooped soup and savoured it. "As good as I remember. Aren't you joining me?"

"I already had dinner, but I'll join you with a glass of wine. Can I pour you one?"

George shook his head. "I have to drive home. Except for the kitchen, the house looks exactly as I remember." He scooped more soup.

"Is that good or bad?" Olivia walked to the refrigerator, reached for the bottle of Zinfandel and poured it into a glass.

"It's good. We shared a lot of memories here."

Olivia stared at the wine in her glass. "We did."

"Do you remember when your mother almost caught us necking on the couch?"

Olivia watched his grin spread. "If I recall correctly, you wanted to do more than that."

"What did you expect? I was a warm-blooded boy with a hot girlfriend. But I didn't get far, and I've lived with the disappointment all these years."

Olivia inclined her head when she felt the flush of heat colour her cheeks.

He liked that she could still be embarrassed easily. An endearing trait that years ago drew him to her. "It's great fate had us running into each other again."

Olivia doubted fate had a hand in their reunion but kept that to herself.

"I wish it were under better circumstances, but it's nice nonetheless." George reached for her hand. The warmth sent shivers up her spine, and she tugged her hand free.

"Would you like another bowl?"

"No, thanks. I better get going. Hopefully, Bob will have a good night." He rose, reached for his bag, and walked toward the front door. "I'll be by in a couple of days. If you need me before then, you have my number."

Olivia wondered if there was a double entendre in his words.

Chapter 25

BOB WASN'T HAVING a good night. The pain was consuming, and his sleep restless. Olivia stayed up with him so Cassie could rest up.

Awake for most of the night, Olivia filled her time by sorting Bob's many drugs and meticulously documenting the administration times and dosages on her laptop. If it came down to Cassie having to give Bob his medication, the file made it simple for her to follow.

It was four in the morning, and the house was quiet aside from Bob's wheezing breaths. Wide awake, and with little else to do, Olivia clicked her book open on the laptop and, picking up where she left off, Olivia typed.

Sucking in air and hissing it out, Olivia pushed off her desk and walked to Catherine's office. Sitting beside Vince at the meeting table, Catherine and he drank coffee and munched on the Italian pastries he brought her.

Catherine gestured for Olivia to take the chair facing them. When Olivia sat, there was no offer of coffee or pastries, only rebuking for not responding to their emails or texts.

"It was my day off. I was dealing with something and didn't have time to respond, nor should I be expected to. Christ, do you people understand the concept of a day off?" If Olivia had a spine, that's what she would say.

Instead, Olivia apologized because arguing with irrational people was stress she didn't need. Olivia had bigger things to deal with than a vain woman searching for validation from the boy toy who lavished her with the craved praise to fulfill his agenda.

"Go ahead and tell Olivia about Scooter Yost, Vince," Catherine said.

"Wooley's buyer?" Olivia said.

"The one and only who you claim is in bed with our competition and refuses to do business with us or take your calls." There wasn't derision in Catherine's voice, but its implication was loud and clear.

"Scooter took my call!" Vince exclaimed, a smug smile settling on his face. "The first and only one I made to him, and he took it. We're paying for his flight and travel expenses to Vietnam and Thailand. That will get us in the door for a further talk with him and net us a good chunk of his business." Vince's thin lips curved into a Joker-like smile. "As I've told you, Olivia, you need to spend money to make money."

Olivia could hear Vince struggling to keep the satisfaction of his magnificent accomplishment from his voice. "You've agreed to this, Catherine?"

Catherine's fire-red painted lips puckered. "Of course I have. As Vince says, you must spend money to make money, Olivia. Scooter's bound to repay the favour."

"He's already agreed to a meeting on his return from his trip," Vince put in.

The look of disbelief in Olivia's eyes was mistaken for regret.

"It's your missed opportunity, Olivia. I've been after you to set up a meeting with Scooter, but you were adamant he wouldn't meet with you." Catherine paused and took a sip of coffee to give Olivia a moment to respond with an apology or possibly an admission of failure to do her job.

The blind leading the arrogant, Olivia thought. Hadn't she told Catherine repeatedly to avoid Scooter's calls asking to fund his travels? Everyone in the business knew Scooter financed his yearly family vacations by tempting gullible suppliers into paying his way across the globe with the promise of business that never came.

"Needless to say, I'll be taking the account over. I know it's your territory, but I think it's only fair I take credit since I did all the legwork." Vince let Olivia drift awhile to sift through the statement, but all that went through Olivia's mind was the thought of how quickly she'd gone from caring about her job to not giving a rat's ass anymore.

"That goes without saying, Vince. Let me know if you need any help." Olivia graciously offered to segue into her request. "I wanted to request to work from home as Vince's salespeople do."

Olivia thought she should have demanded, not asked, watching them mull the answer. When she thought they would turn her down, she played the card she hoped not to.

"My sister is sick, and it would be easier to care for her if I could work from home." Olivia's face softened in the hope it would trigger a positive response, and she felt sick she had to play it out this way.

This was what her life was now.

"We're sorry about your sister, Olivia, and of course, you can work from home for as long as you need. You have our full support, right Catherine," Vince said with feigned compassion in his eyes.

"Of course, Olivia, take all the time you need, and if you need anything from us, let us know."

Olivia wasn't expecting support, let alone sympathy. Smiling faintly, she stared at them with a suspicious eye.

Olivia read and decided what she wrote wasn't the making of a sellable book. What she wrote was an outline to be revisited when her mind wasn't too tired or filled with worry brought on by Bob's circumstances to put a coherent thought together.

Olivia heard Lottie say, "I told you so," in her head.

But Olivia couldn't help but worry. She worried about Bob's impending death and Cassie being left alone. She worried about administering Bob's drugs wrongly. Olivia worried the nurse, Lottie, scheduled to arrive mid-morning, wouldn't show up or that Cassie would become territorial and not approve of her caring for Bob.

Olivia worried about everything and couldn't think straight. She was reliving the whirlwind of debilitating emotions she endured through the years of caring for her mother all over again.

Olivia checked on Bob. The Fentanyl did its job, and Bob slept peacefully.

Setting the coffee to brew in the kitchen, Olivia deleted the text message from Lottie, the fourth since seeing George, asking for the scoop. She would call Lottie later and disappoint her. The feel-good story Lottie wanted to hear from Olivia about her and George didn't exist. George was Bob's neurologist, and that was the extent of their connection.

The coffeemaker muttered when it finished brewing coffee into the pot and scented the air. Olivia filled her cup, added cream and sugar and sipped deep before turning the heat on the frying pan. Bacon and scrambled eggs were on the menu for breakfast this morning.

Chapter 26

OLIVIA'S WORRY WAS unwarranted. The nurse Lottie contracted showed up at ten-thirty as scheduled. Rose was a sixty-ish, boisterous woman with a bright, wide smile. Her eyes were as dark as her smooth skin. She wore a blue dress with a round white collar and large pockets at the waist. Cassie immediately took a liking to Rose.

Rose introduced herself to Bob and went to work. She expressed no shock at his condition, nor did she minimize him or treat him like an invalid. She changed Bob's bedsheet, gave him a sponge bath, and dressed him in clean pyjamas. Rose administered medications and replaced Bob's IV drip. With Cassie's assistance, Rose tended to all of Bob's medical needs efficiently and professionally. Including Cassie in her father's care was integral to acceptance, and Rose understood that.

Cassie fed Bob what little broth he could eat while Olivia made lunch and Rose did a load of laundry. Between the three—mostly Rose—Olivia was confident they could care for Bob. One less thing to worry about.

"You're all right with Rose taking care of Bob, Cassie." Olivia moved the banker's box against the wall to clear a pathway for Rose.

"Yeah, she's been great. She knows what she's doing and doesn't treat Dad like a sick person, you know."

"Yes, I know."

"Maybe I'll consider becoming a nurse. I like to help people, you know. Do you want this packed?" Cassie asked. At Olivia's nod, she picked up the vase with fake flowers at the center of the table. "This is nice," she said, packing it into the box.

Olivia shot Cassie a smile. "Don't say that in front of Lottie. She thinks everything in this house should be buried in a time capsule to be opened thousands of years into the future."

"Why?"

"Lottie is the modern-look type."

"But isn't this stuff your parents?" Cassie reached for the bevelled glass ashtray and wrapped it in the newspaper.

"It is, but Lottie's not the sentimental type. She thinks the old needs to be left in the past, especially if it brings up bad memories. That ashtray was my father's. He was a chain smoker, and it was constantly jammed-packed with butts. The excessive smoking eventually contributed to his death, and Lottie would rather not have the reminder."

"I guess some people are like that. My mom was like that. She wanted to forget, and she did."

To Olivia's disappointment, Cassie left it there, and she didn't ask the questions on her mind. The talk about Cassie's mother had to be approached with care. Olivia understood she and Cassie needed to have a stronger connection than Bob for her to delve into Cassie's life to quell her curiosity. They weren't there yet.

"I'm glad you like Rose. It's important you do," Olivia said.

"I do. She's sassy, and Dad needs sassy to put him in his place. You know, he's strong-willed."

"He is that."

"Anyway, I love her hair. She told me she could braid my hair into cornrows if I want."

"Food for thought."

"Huh." Cassie's confused gaze rested a moment on Olivia.

"It warrants some serious consideration."

"Oh. Yeah, I'm thinking about it. My hair is thin, not as luscious and thick as Rose's." Cassie sealed the box with tape and set it on top of the one against the wall. "I do envy her boobs, though."

Olivia sputtered out a laugh. "Really, Cassie."

"You laugh, but I know you do too. I mean, look at us with our tiny boobies. She must be a triple D."

"Oh, no, Rose is the off-scale cup size," Olivia said, and both snorted a laugh. "Do you think Bob likes Rose?"

"I'm sure he does, but honestly, I think he's more interested that someone's helping us out. He didn't want to be such a burden on us." Cassie set Bob's medications on the table in the sequence Rose specified on her notes.

"Good, because I told Rose to schedule herself for a full shift from tomorrow onward. She suggested we bring Bonita in for the night shift. Bonita's coming today at six. We'll meet her then. Between them and us, Bob will have round-the-clock care."

"Sounds good." Cassie looked up at Olivia. "You need to let me pay for all this. I have the two hundred dollars in my backpack, and I can get more."

"As Lottie said, you don't need to worry about that," Olivia assured Cassie. She wouldn't come to know that two hundred dollars wouldn't put a dent in Bob's medical bill. "She and I will take care of everything."

"Pay it forward. I remember."

"Yeah, well, I think we're almost set up here. This will be Bob central. His drugs, laundry, change of pyjamas, and everything Bob will be on this table for easy access. And when things are quiet, I'll work on my book from here. It'll keep me close to Bob so I can keep an eye on him." They both turned in Bob's direction when they heard him gasp. He fell back into sleep.

"Fentanyl is a wonderful drug," Olivia said. "Malcolm from my ex-workplace will be by later to help get the television from my bedroom installed on the wall so Bob can watch TV." Olivia handed Cassie the mouse and pad to set next to her laptop on the table. "Sondra, another work colleague, will come along for the ride. She's trying to get him to fall in love with her. I thought we could have a BBQ out on the patio. Would you like that?"

Cassie nodded. "That sounds good. It's been a long while since I visited with anyone."

"I thought you might like company closer to your age. Malcolm is a few years older than you are, but being a guy, he acts more like a child."

That got a snorting giggle from Cassie. "My mom used to say something like that."

"She sounds like a smart woman."

"She was."

"I've invited Lottie and the girls," Olivia said, breaking the silence. "Adam, Lottie's husband, is in New York on business, and my sister's idea of cooking is dialling for pizza. I hope you're okay with that."

Cassie nodded. "It sounds like fun."

"I'm glad you think so because you're going to help prep."

"Prep?"

"We'll make a salad. I thought a potato would do. Everyone likes potatoes. And a regular garden salad for those opposed to carbs. I have ground meat, which we'll make into hamburgers and hot dogs."

"What about dessert?" Cassie's voice was ripe with excitement this time.

"I didn't think about dessert." Olivia thought. "I'll have Sondra pick up a chocolate-chip ice cream cake on her way here. Everyone loves ice cream."

"And chocolate, I know I do." Cassie's face beamed with a smile. "Do you mind if I take the vase that was on the table? I want to set it next to Dad's bed and fill it with some real flowers from the garden. I thought they'd cheer him up."

"I don't mind at all. It's a nice idea. After we finish prepping, I'll help you cut the flowers."

"Thank you, Olivia." Cassie's green eyes on blue, she exchanged a look of appreciation with Olivia for giving her a sense of family and making her feel a part of one.

"You're very welcome, Cassie." Olivia softened her voice when she answered.

The girl was reaching into Olivia's heart and tethering herself to it. Olivia heard Lottie's voice in her head.

She's not your daughter, Olivia. You're not responsible for the girl. You need to get off this emotional train to crazy town and get your emotions under control before it becomes too late. Once Bob is gone, Cassie may also be gone, and where does that leave you?

And Lottie was right, but how could Olivia discount Cassie, who reminded her of Lottie and her difficulty in dealing with their mother's illness and death?

Chapter 27

CASSIE DRAGGED THE spread over her sleeping father. "I like your nieces. They're smart and nice and so pretty."

"They like you too." Olivia arranged the blue irises in the vase next to Bob's bed. Cassie was right to think they would light up the room.

"And your friends are funny and fun." Cassie handed Olivia the glass of water to pour into the vase.

"Yes, Sondra and Malcolm are a hoot."

"Dad enjoyed visiting with them and sitting outside in the sunlight, even if it was for a few minutes. And he enjoyed that brownie Sondra gave him. It's the first time I've seen him eat and not feel nauseous afterward. They're magical."

"Yes, magical, but medicinal." Olivia pointed out. "They're medicinal. You didn't have any, did you?"

Cassie shook her head. "Sondra said she made them for Dad." With a tender touch, Cassie ran a hand over Bob's forehead.

Olivia started to talk and stopped when she thought she heard Bonita come out of the bathroom to join them. When Bonita didn't appear, Olivia said, "She did make them for Bob, and that'll be our secret. Okay?"

"Okay. She left me three brownies and told me to give them to Dad when he's having a bad day. She said if I needed more, to let her know."

"That's our Sondra, always accommodating."

"I told her I'd contribute to the cost of the pot she uses, and she turned me down."

Olivia cast startled blue eyes at Cassie. "You knew."

"Christ, I knew?" Bonita's booming voice startled them when she walked into the living room. The white uniform against her coffee-coloured skin matched the all-perfect-teeth dazzling smile she flashed. Her hair was tightly tied into a round bun, and her waistline was as large as her personality. Her almond-shaped eyes were the type that looked as if they were always smiling.

"Shit," Olivia said under her breath.

"Shit is right. Honey, I have six children and twelve grandchildren and developed superpower hearing over the years. And you honestly thought I wouldn't notice how blissful Bob was after he ate the brownie?"

"I'm sorry. It won't happen again." Guilt and shame flashed on Olivia's face.

"No, it won't, not on my watch." She waved a stiff finger in the air at Olivia and Cassie. "But what happens in this house when I'm not here is beyond my control," Bonita commented with a wink.

"Thanks, Bonita. Come help me clean up in the kitchen." Olivia reached for Cassie's hand and led her out of the living room.

"Did Bonita just say we can give Dad the brownies behind her back?"

Olivia nodded. "With the underlying message, we tell no one."

"Mum's the word. Thank Sondra for me and tell her I think she and Malcolm make a cute couple." Cassie collected the dirty dishes on the table and handed them to

Olivia to run a soapy sponge over them. "What about this book you want to write?"

Olivia ran the dishes under water to rinse them. "Sondra has a big mouth?"

"Don't get mad at Sondra. You mentioned it but didn't go into detail, and I asked her about it. Sondra told me it's a dream of yours." Cassie set dirty cutlery into the soapy water.

"I can never get mad at Sondra. The book is something I've always wanted to do, but it's more or less on the back burner for now."

"Because of Dad?"

Olivia dried her hands on the dish towel. "To be honest, it's not coming together."

"Because of all the drama, we brought to your life."

Moving across the kitchen floor to the stove, Olivia hung the dish towel on the handle to dry. "That's part of it."

"What's the other part," Cassie prodded when Olivia went contemplative.

"I'm finding writing more difficult than I imagined it to be. In my head, the concept sounds good, but when I transfer my thoughts into words, it doesn't come together. I don't feel it." Olivia admitted after a moment's hesitation.

Cassie put the last dish away. "Maybe you need to pour yourself into your story. You know, not just tell a story, but throw all of your emotion into it," Cassie said matter-of-factly.

Olivia thought that nothing had ever sounded as perfect as those words. That was what she was missing.

Chapter 28

LATER, WHEN CASSIE was asleep with Oreo in her arms and Bob under Bonita's watchful eye, Olivia showered the day away under the spray of hot water. Towel drying her hair, she went through her body moisturizing routine. Olivia threw on her comfortable oversized nightgown and walked to her bedroom.

She slid the window open to let air into the room. It was a cool, clear night. The scents of lilac and moist earth from Mr. Buchanan's recently watered grass poured into the room. In the darkness of the night, everything beyond the window looked peaceful. It suited her mood.

Cassie enjoyed the BBQ. Being surrounded by family and friends gave Cassie a sense of home, family, and hope, which was Olivia's intention.

Olivia didn't know Cassie's story, who her mother was, or how she came to connect with Bob. Olivia didn't know much—yet. The one thing Olivia knew was that Cassie loved Bob and soon would be numb with grief, feeling lost and alone. Cassie needed a home now and more so after Bob left this earth. Olivia recognized Cassie's need for a family to call her own and a home to make her feel safe and wanted was critical to helping her navigate the difficult days ahead.

Once again, Olivia was back at that forked road.

The right thing to do was to take Cassie into her home and be the family she needed. But being responsible for another human requires commitment. Aside from the emotional component Cassie would be dealing with for years, there was the financial one and a difficult one for Olivia to meet. Olivia could barely take care of herself, let alone another human being.

Olivia set those thoughts aside and walked to her bed.

Sitting back in her bed Olivia turned her laptop on. With Cassie's words in mind, she made notes on the day's events. Olivia wrote about the evening BBQ, Lottie, the girls, Sondra, Malcolm, and Cassie. Emotions bottled inside for months poured out with every word.

Olivia wrote and wrote, disengaging her emotional gears. Before Olivia knew it, the new day's light dawned on the horizon.

After all these months, Olivia found her writing voice.

Chapter 29

CASSIE STEPPED BACK to let Dr. Papa in and escorted him to the living room. "Dad's been doing way better. It's like he's a new man. Like he's getting better. Isn't that true, Daddy?" Cassie asked when they walked into the living room.

The bed was raised to allow Bob to watch the television. An episode of Law & Order played on the television, Malcolm had mounted on the swivelling arm. His skin seemed to have some colour, and he had a joyful smile.

Bob flicked his eyes, more alert than George had seen in a long while, in his direction. "Absolutely right, pumpkin. I feel great." His voice was faint but cheery.

"Hello, Bob." George set his medical bag on the table. "I have to say you do look good."

Bob flashed a wider smile at that. "It's been a while since I've felt this good."

"So those cannabis-laced brownies are doing wonders." George reached into his bag for the stethoscope and listened to Bob's chest.

"Bonita told. She said she wouldn't tell." Cassie picked Oreo up to stop him from barking. "Shh, Oreo, Dr. Papa needs to listen to Daddy's chest."

When Oreo wouldn't stop yapping, George gave him a gentle ear scratch. "Yes, I know you're here, Oreo." That silenced Oreo and garnered George a grin. "Bonita told me she didn't see anything," George air quoted the words, "but wanted to check with me if you and Olivia considered it an ongoing occurrence. You know, to make sure it was okay. I told her it was."

"Good because it's made Daddy feel better than all those pills, Dr. Papa."

"For the record, I don't make the brownies. I have a supplier," Olivia said, walking into the conversation. She wore a sunny yellow flowing blouse tucked into the copper-brown capris. Her hair, a cloud of chestnut, flowed around the unpainted face George thought hadn't been touched by time or the struggles that she had faced in her life. "That didn't come out right. My friend makes them and supplies them for Bob's use."

The scent of her lavender soap reached him when she stood by him and stirred something in George he hadn't felt in a long while. He caught himself staring at Olivia and put a few inches of distance between them.

"Well, ah, you, umm, don't need to feel guilty." George stammered.

"That's right. Medicinal cannabis is not against the law." Bonita entered the living room and joined the circle around Bob's bed. "I had to ensure it wouldn't interfere with Bob's meds." With her hands on her hips, Bonita eyed George. "You all right, Dr. Papa? You look a bit flushed."

Regaining his composure, George said, "It's been a long day, and you were right, Bonita, for checking with me. It's better to be safe than sorry. This is the one time I'm glad my patient did something behind my back. Doctors don't prescribe cannabis for pain management, but we're not against our patients experimenting with it. At least I'm not. Most often than not, the results of cannabis use by patients like Bob have good results. Ultimately the patient's comfort is what it's about."

"Good, because I'm not giving up my brownies," Bob put in as Law & Order's familiar dum-dum pierced the conversation.

"Now, everyone out." Bonita handed George her medical notes. "Dr. Papa needs a few minutes with Bob to give him a look-see."

Cassie slid an arm through the crook of Olivia's. Sure, okay. Dr. Papa, will you join us for dinner? Olivia made lasagna and Caesar salad. She's an excellent cook, you know." Cassie looked away when Olivia furrowed her brows.

"I'm sure she is." Dr. Papa read Bonita's notes.

"There's also garlic bread," Cassie added when she thought George was searching for the words to refuse her invitation.

"How can I pass that up?"

"We'll set another place at the table. Join us in the kitchen when you're done." Cassie offered a dimpled grin.

"Take the dog with you," Bonita demanded, and before Cassie could command Oreo to follow them, he scampered from the room.

"He knows who's boss," said George.

"Damn straight,"

CASSIE SUDDENLY WASN'T HUNGRY, AND NEITHER was Bonita, and both left Olivia and George to enjoy dinner together on the patio under a setting sun.

The air smelled floral and strong. A warm breeze rustled the leaves on the maple, shading them, and cicadas serenaded. From somewhere, a frog croaked, and his companion answered as Mr. Dawg from next door barked. The round wrought iron table was fancily made up, with a linen tablecloth, napkins, Olivia's best crystal, and two roses from the garden in the middle.

"I'm sorry, George, but I suspect Cassie is trying her hand at matchmaking. You don't have to stay if you don't want to." In the morning, Olivia would have a word with Cassie. As well-meaning as the attempt was, boundaries needed to be set. Besides, George was married, and Cassie's efforts would lead to nothing.

"Yes, I gathered that, but no, I don't want to leave unless, of course, you want me to."

Olivia shook her head. "I'd like you to stay."

"Can I tempt you into a glass of wine? One drink with dinner is not going to hurt any." After some prodding, he agreed to a glass of wine and looked as relaxed as Olivia.

George shed his suit jacket, removed his tie, and unbuttoned the top two buttons of his shirt. They ate delicious food, talked, reminisced, and enjoyed each other's company.

Olivia had to admit it was nice to have a man, a friend nonetheless, to talk with. She'd long forgotten what it was like to spend a few hours in the company of a man she liked.

One hour passed into two, and before they knew it, night had fallen. Above, the moon was sliced in half, its glow sharp in the dark sky coalesced with million stars that filled it.

Olivia and George cleared the dishes. Olivia washed, and George dried. Olivia put away the dried pots, plates, and cutlery while George stacked the leftover containers in the refrigerator. She got the coffee and filter from the pantry while he poured water into the coffee maker's reservoir.

George anticipated her every move, her every step and she, his. Synergy, Olivia thought. That was the true meaning of the word.

The coffee brewed and poured, and Olivia led George outside to the patio. Each took a seat at the Muskoka chairs.

In the back of her mind, the thought of why George felt no urgency to go home to his wife lingered, but she tucked it away. Right or wrong, she didn't want him to leave.

"It's a beautiful night." George stretched his legs out and crossed his feet at the ankles.

"Until winter rears its head, Oreo and I sit out here for hours." The night breeze whiffled through her hair, and he had to draw on all his strength not to reach out and tuck the loose strands behind her ear. "I love the fall when…."

"The leaves, burned gold and crimson, on the trees flutter in the crisp fall wind," George finished. Now he smiled that huge ray of light that had brightened Olivia every day of their time together and sent her heart doing the quick gallop she hadn't felt in so long. Olivia said nothing, only stared at George with those mesmerizing blue eyes. "Yes, I remember, Olivia. I remember lots of things," he said and flying back over time into memories of their time together, they fell into a companionable silence.

"Cassie thinks Bob's getting better, but you know it's the temporary euphoric feeling from the brownie making him feel better."

"I know." Olivia sipped at her coffee.

"I'll have to talk to her and present the facts."

Olivia cast her eyes on the sky. All she could think was how radiant and mysterious it looked. "Not yet. Bob's dying. There's nothing we can do about that, but we can make her last few days with him a memorable time for her." Olivia turned to George. "Please, George, Bob's the only family she has; she doesn't have much time left with him."

George nodded. "All right, but sooner or later, I will have to talk with her."

"I know."

Silence fell between them once again.

"What you're doing for Bob and Cassie, Olivia, is admirable."

"What we're doing, George. I mean, you agreed to take him as a patient. You didn't have to do that. Bob wasn't the nicest person to you. Aside from coming between us, his bullying and shaming because of what your father did for a living was inexcusable."

"Clinging to Anger is not a good feeling, and to carry it with you is unproductive. It saps your energy and creativity. It consumes you."

She rolled that in her head for a moment.

"Not that I'm grateful for what Bob did, but I think it made me stronger and pushed me to succeed. Experience can inform or distort. I chose to go the inform route and decided to become a doctor," George explained.

Olivia gave her a faint smile. "You chose well since you're not just any doctor. You're a published neurologist sought out to speak on your work targeting the progression of brain tumours."

"You've been reading my bio on the hospital's website."

"I have, and I'm proud of you, George. Frankly, I didn't think you were so smart," she said with humour in her eyes.

George threw back his head and laughed. "Well, one thing Bob did right," George reached for her hand, "was bring us back together."

Olivia turned to him with a smile and slowly linked her fingers with his. They remained this way long into the night.

Part III

The End

In the end, we all become memories. Leave ones worth remembering.

—M.L. Lexi

Chapter 30

SONDRA FELT IT essential she kept Olivia abreast with the goings-on in the office, and she and Malcolm showed up at her front door. Cassie answered the door. She wore short khaki overalls against a brown tank top and white tennis shoes. Her hair flowed straight around her face. Her face had a lovely summer bronze colour to it.

Cassie's smile was huge when she saw them. "Hi, guys." She leaned in for a hug.

"Oh, okay, yeah, I forgot you're a hugger," Malcolm's hand floated mid-air while his nervous eyes remained on Sondra.

"Hey, Cass, is Olivia in?" Sondra pulled back from the embrace. "This is for your dad." She handed the Tupperware of brownies to Cassie.

"Thanks, and Olivia's in the kitchen making dinner." Cassie stepped aside to let them in. "You have to be quiet. Daddy's resting, and you don't want Bonita on your ass."

Nodding, Sondra walked past Cassie. "It smells great in here," she murmured.

"Roast chicken with carrots and something called fingerling potatoes. We have enough if you'd like to stay for dinner." Cassie followed Sondra past the hallway to the kitchen.

"Maybe, love, but I need to talk to Olivia right now."

"Talk to Olivia about what?" Olivia looked up when Sondra appeared at the door.

The early evening sun spilling through the window was dazzling. Next to the cutting board on the counter, potato, carrot, onion, and garlic peels were stacked high. In a bamboo bowl, chopped lettuce with cucumber slices and tomato sat ready to be dressed. The table was set for three.

"Lots was going on in the office today that you will be pleased to hear about, and I rushed over to tell you." Sondra reached for a carrot and crunched it between her teeth.

The smile in Sondra's eyes told Olivia she was about to add to the high she'd been riding on all day from her night with George.

Olivia and George hadn't gone past the holding hand stage, but the giddy schoolgirl, butterflies in the stomach, feeling from last night still lingered in her. The little things bring the most pleasure.

If Cassie, Bob, and Bonita hadn't been at home, Olivia was sure she would have walked George to her bedroom and done what she vowed never to do to another woman. She had been at the receiving end of Bob's cheating more times than she cared to admit, and it had sapped her dignity and the woman she was.

Olivia swore never to put any woman through that, but last night she came close to breaking her oath by taking married George to bed.

When George reached for her hand, its warmth clouded her mind. For an instant, logic and reason went out the door. Olivia then wanted to have George in her bed touching her body, making her feel like a woman loved. But Cassie, Bob, and Bonita forced Olivia to shelve the temptation rearing in her.

"Spill." Olivia sat, and a curious Cassie followed suit.

"Tell her, Malcolm." Sondra popped the last of the carrot into her mouth.

"Well, talk, Malcolm. Now," Olivia demanded.

"How come you don't talk to Sondra that way?" Malcolm reached into the Tupperware container, tore a piece of brownie and tossed it back.

"Talk, Malcolm." Olivia and Sondra said simultaneously.

Malcolm swallowed. "Vince asked me to give him access to your emails and address book and all your files."

The room went quiet, and everyone's eyes cut from Malcolm to Olivia, who stared dully. In the past, Olivia's first reaction would have been panic and rage, and the angst that followed would choke her, and her mind would race to every adverse scenario she could fabricate.

Not today, Olivia decided as George's words rolled in her head: Clinging to Anger is not a good feeling, and to carry it with you is unproductive. It saps your energy and creativity. It consumes you.

"Efficient as always, our Vince. I've been gone for months, and he's only now getting around to mining my laptop," Olivia said.

The calm in Olivia's voice made Sondra's lips curve into a smile. "Olive Oyl, you have the Dr. Evil sneer on your face. What did you do?"

"Who's Olive Oyl?" Cassie asked.

"It's some old folk reference." Malcolm's comment got him a stern look from Sondra.

Olivia rose and got four glasses from the cupboard. She got the lemon-peach-flavoured water she had made for dinner from the refrigerator, calmly poured it into the glasses and set them before each. "Let me explain."

When Malcolm was around Sondra and Olivia, he always needed a pick-me-up, and he reached into the Tupperware for another brownie. "Hey, I wanted that," he said when Sondra snapped the lid on the container and slid it across the table to Cassie.

"Those are for Bob," she said to Malcolm and then turned to Olivia. "Hurry up with the explanation already."

"You are an impatient one." Olivia walked to the pantry and reached for the box of glazed donuts. "You underestimate me, but I'm no longer the old Olivia."

"What does that mean?" said Sondra. "Stop talking in riddles, woman, and tell me already."

Oliva handed Malcolm the donuts. "Here, an appetizer slash bribe."

Now Malcolm said, "What are you talking about?"

"I anticipated Vince would ask Malcolm to comb through my laptop. When Vincent and Catherine became supportive and understanding, I knew something was up. So, I deleted files and saved others. The same goes for my contacts and emails. I mined the database, downloaded information to my USB, and manipulated much of the contact data. I wasn't handing over all that data and making life easy for Vincent and Elvira. They can find the contact information by doing their job as I did."

Sondra's face went brilliant with pleasure. "You are in danger of becoming a fascinating woman. Respect, Olive Oyl." Sondra stood and bowed before Olivia.

"Who's this Olive Oyl she keeps mentioning?" Cassie asked.

"No one worth knowing," Malcolm said with a mouthful of donuts. "And for the record, Olivia, I'm impressed."

"Christ, do you need to shove an entire donut in your mouth?" Sondra retorted. "It's not an attractive look."

"You like it when…."

"Children in the room, and by that, I mean Olivia, not you, Cassie." Sondra stopped Malcolm from finishing the thought.

Cassie sputtered a laugh while Olivia simply arched her eyebrows. "I'm not just a pretty face, Malcolm." Olivia handed him a paper towel. "And I like to thank you for your help."

"Shit." Malcolm swallowed the contents in his mouth. "What are you talking about?"

"What is she talking about? Why is she thanking you for your help, Malcolm?" Sondra eyed him sharply like a bear at mealtime. "You knew what was going down, and you let me go on and on in the car ride here."

"Help me out here, Olivia. Otherwise, this won't end here."

"Don't blame Malcolm, Sondra. I asked him not to tell you. I didn't want to get you involved. I told Malcolm to give Vince and Catherine everything he found but not to admit to any deleted information. Vincent is as inept with the computer as Catherine, and he'd never find anything missing."

"Pfft, that was easy enough. I always do that for the guys who take their laptops home." Malcolm shoved another donut into his mouth, and Sondra and Olivia's faces puckered in disgust while Cassie's filled with a smile. "You should see some of the shit these guys watch at home on their laptops."

"Everyone has their limits, and I reached mine. The evil you can concoct when you're pushed to the edge is remarkable. I had enough of their bullshit, and this is part of the retaliation I came up with against Vince."

There's no power better than that which you allow yourself to take.

Being in control of her life felt empowering, a liberating experience. The knot of stress tangled with anger loosened for the first time in a long while. The bitterness weighing Olivia down all these years melted away, and her work-related anger all at once felt trivial and meaningless. Suddenly, Vince, Catherine, and everyone who had a hand in making Olivia's life a wretched hell seemed inconsequential.

Mouth, agape, Sondra stared at Olivia. "Slow clap to that, Olive Oyl. You said part of the retaliation. What's the rest?"

"I called a couple of the sales competitors I like and provided them with the information of my top contracts, suppliers, price, and all the necessary data for them to take the business from Sullivan's."

Sondra brought her hands together and proceeded to slow clap. "Well done."

"Even I was impressed with her deviousness. I didn't think saintly Olivia had it in her." Malcolm licked the donut glaze off his fingers.

"Don't think your smart mouth is getting you off the hook, mister. If you want to continue getting a sweet taste of this," Sondra skimmed fingers up and down her body, "you better tell me everything, and I mean everything, from here on," Sondra said and made Cassie and Olivia snort a giggle.

Chapter 31

GEORGE'S VISITS TO the house became more frequent, and although the war between Olivia's conscience and morality raged, she didn't push George away and didn't object to his extended stays after he had checked on Bob. Olivia didn't discourage George when he told her he wanted to spend more time getting to know her.

George was a married man, and Olivia was going to hell.

But it wasn't as if she walked him to her bedroom and had him sliding into her bed as she ached to do. As much as she wanted to lock lips with him, Olivia hadn't. She put distance between them the few times she'd seen the yearning to kiss her in his eyes.

George made her heart swell, and the slow, liquid warmth spread in her belly, but Olivia never crossed the invisible but undeniable line of morality. Olivia would never betray another woman. Thinking and doing were very different things. She and George were friends, and she'd never cross the line beyond friendship.

As for Cassie, there was still a lot Olivia didn't know, but she'd slid into Lottie's and her heart. Lottie saw Cassie as a sister, and Olivia saw her as the daughter Bob refused to give her. Cassie was loving, warm, and good company. She filled the house with youthful life, energy, and laughter, something Olivia's home lacked for so long.

Olivia's days, however, weren't all cheerful.

As the days slid by, Bob didn't get better. Sondra's brownies gave Bob the relief his medication couldn't, but they also deluded Cassie into believing Bob's health was improving. Olivia decided it was time George talked with Cassie. Cassie needed to hear the truth about Bob's deteriorating state. Cassie had to prepare herself for the inevitable, which according to George, was days, possibly hours away.

Olivia set her wine glass on the table. "It's time Cassie's told the truth, Bob. She loves you so much she doesn't want to let you go, and she's diluted herself into believing you're getting better. If she's not told the truth, it will be more difficult for her to deal with your loss. She will hate you, me, and become jaded. Time is the great balm. Her pain will smooth out one day, but until then, it's not a good place to be at a young age. I thought I'd get George to talk to her." Olivia buttoned Bob's pyjama shirt, now twice too big for him. Bob had lost weight over the past weeks, and nothing fit his thin body properly. He was fading away before her eyes. "I should get you some new pyjamas."

"Don't bother. There won't be any need for them soon."

Olivia looked at him. "Don't talk like that, Bob."

"I've made peace with my death, Olivia. I'm ready for it. I'm tired, physically and mentally. Believe it or not, I want the end to come. This is no way to live for me and you, certainly not Cassie."

Olivia reached for his bony hand and enveloped it with hers. "I don't mind, really I don't, and I know Cassie doesn't either."

Hollowed eyes shifted and met Olivia's. "You've been good to me, Olivia, better than I deserve, then and now."

"I won't argue with that," she replied with a soft smile before she turned to slide the curtains close to a clear, starry night.

"I can only say I'm sorry and thank you for everything you've done for me, Olivia, for what Lottie has done. I never thought she'd be as helpful as she has been." Bob watched the television screen go dark when she turned it off.

"I won't lie, neither did I, and you've already thanked her and me." Olivia slid the bed cover to his neck. "You should get some sleep."

"I'll talk to Cassie about my deteriorating health. I want to," he added when she started to speak.

"All right, but I should be with her when you do."

"All right." Bob stared at Olivia through tired eyes. "You've come to care for Cassie."

"She's easy to like. Cassie's a lovely girl, caring, loving, and honest. You should be proud of your daughter."

"She is all that." Bob was silent for a moment as he gathered his strength to continue. The hum of the air conditioner turning on underlined the heavy silence. "She's not my daughter," he said after some time. Bob read the knowledge in Olivia's eyes. "But you knew that already."

She nodded. "I suspected it, but I wasn't one hundred percent sure. However minute, there was the possibility you had reversed the vasectomy you got when we were together."

He shook his head.

"Yeah, I didn't think so. You were adamant about not having children. So, how did Cassie come about?"

"She showed up on my front door one day." He stopped for breath.

"Take your time."

"She flashes her birth certificate, which has my name and says she's my daughter."

Olivia cocked her head. "And cynical, selfish, narcissist, you believed every word and took her in, just like that."

His laughter became a coughing fit. Olivia brought the straw to his lips. "I deserve that." He sipped water to lubricate his throat. She looked dishevelled, thin, and lost. She said her mother told her just before she died I was her father. I knew the chances of that were zero, but she told me she had nowhere to go and no money. I told her she could stay for the night. One night turned into days and weeks, and she grew on me in the interim. I suddenly liked being called Daddy."

Olivia turned as Bonita came into the room, nibbling on an oatmeal cookie. "We need a few more minutes, Bonita." Bonita hesitated for a moment. "Please."

"All right, ten minutes, then I need to give Bob his meds, and he needs to rest." Bonita waved a stern sausage-thick finger at Olivia.

"Yes, ma'am."

When they were alone again, Bob continued. "When my mother met Cassie, it was instant love. She saw the change in me, the responsible man I'd become. Cassie made me the man I never was, and my mother tells me she's the best thing I've done in my life and made me promise to 'get my shit together and take care of my daughter.'"

"Your mother always had a way with words. Did you ever tell her the truth?" Olivia watched Bob's eyes focus on some distant point as if drawing on a memory.

"I didn't get the chance. She went and died on me before I could. An aneurysm took her without warning. For good or bad, Mom was the only person always on my side no matter what I did."

Olivia thought she saw a solitary tear track a line down his cheek. "I'm sorry, Bob."

"I'm just glad she died before she could see me in this state." Bob stared at Olivia. "There's a favour I need to ask of you. It's a big one, but you're my last resort."

His eyes were serious, probing, and she said. "If I can."

"I want you to take care of Cassie when I'm gone. She has no one and has had too much heartbreak and disappointment in her life. She's a beautiful person and deserves happiness and love to fill her life, and I know you'll give her both."

Olivia stared at him with a thoughtful, narrowed-eye look. That Bob could care about someone more than he did himself, staggered her. Cassie shaped Bob's life in ways no one else had. The power of a child's love could move tectonic plates and bring continents together.

"There's no payment, no gesture that comes close to repaying you for everything you've done for me, and I know it's a lot to ask, Olivia, but I have no one else to turn to. I have some money, and there's the insurance money for which you're the beneficiary." Olivia's eyes fixed wide in shock. "Yes, Olivia, there's insurance money to which you're the beneficiary. It's meant to cover the debt I left you with interest. I thought you'd appreciate the poetic justice."

"Christ, Bob, you always had a flair for the dramatic."

"Drama is my middle name. Look at me now. I couldn't just go out without a bang. I had to linger, and linger, deteriorating in pain. I guess karma had to have the last word," he said with a grin. "So, will you do it, Olivia? Will you raise my daughter as your own? Will you teach her how to be the kind of woman you are? I want her to grow up to be as strong as you are. I want her to be the fearless woman you are."

"I'm not strong and certainly not fearless, Bob."

"You've always underestimated yourself, Olivia. You survived my tyrant way and surfaced from the murky water I left you drowning in to protect Lottie and your home. You took your life back, put Lottie through school, and made her who she is today. You, Olivia, are fearless and tenfold the human being I ever was. That's the woman I want raising my daughter."

The words tinged with genuine sincerity gave Olivia a hard knock to her chest, and her throat choked up. Yet another layer of the Bob-onion she didn't think existed peeled away.

"It would be my honour to bring Cassie into the fold of my home, Bob. I will do everything necessary to ensure she has a happy home with me."

"Thank you, Olivia. I'll leave it up to you to tell her the truth. I rather she never knew she's not my daughter, but in due course, she will need to know."

Olivia nodded. "I'll cross that bridge when it needs crossing."

"One last thing, Olivia. You may face some hostility from my sister. Michelle never accepted Cassie. My sister is a suspicious, untrusting woman, and I'm sure she suspects Cassie isn't my daughter. My mother left me the family house, which I leave to Cassie, amongst other things, and I know Michelle will fight Cassie for it. She fought me tooth and nail for the house but lost. She believes she deserves everything, Huntley, and I should get nothing." Bob's voice started sounding fatigued, and he paused for a moment.

"There's a will. Cassie knows where it is. Still, Michelle's very much like my father. She's intimidating, and a formidable adversary, but so are you, Olivia. Protect Cassie from Michelle."

Hearing the urgency in his tone, Olivia kept her eyes direct on him and vowed, "I will, Bob. I promise you."

Her pledge made, Bob relaxed. "Good. Now, I think a drink is in order." Olivia arched dark brows. "A taste then. It's been so long since I had a drink."

Olivia picked up her wine glass and plucked the straw from Bob's water glass. Bringing the straw to his lips, she watched him slurp wine.

"Whiskey would be better, but Christ, that's good."

Olivia allowed him another sip. "If George finds out I'm doing this, he will not be happy with me."

"George can never be angry with you. He's in love with you," Bob said, and Olivia reacted by tugging the straw from his mouth. "He's in love with you, still."

Olivia eased away from the bed. "He's a married man."

"He hasn't told you." Bob rolled his eyes dramatically when her brows knit in confusion. "Christ, you two haven't changed. Years passed, and you still can't talk openly."

"What are you talking about? What hasn't he told me?"

"He told you his wife is a pediatric oncologist."

"Yes, he told me. He also told me she's retired."

Bob breathed deeply for breath. "That's what he calls it."

Olivia slanted a confused look Bob's way. "If not retired, what is she?"

"Pediatric oncology is an emotionally demanding specialty. You know, dealing with dying children is not easy. After twenty years of practice, she had an emotional breakdown." Bob watched Olivia pay closer attention now as the story spooled out. "George got her the best help, but her mind, simply put, checked out from living. In the end, reluctantly, he admitted her. She's been in a mental health facility for some time."

She opened her mouth, and her eyes widened. "He never said." Olivia's heart sank deep in her chest. That sweet, caring George had to navigate through such difficulty and endure the devastating heartbreak he had made her heart weep for him. You never truly know what anyone has been through or going through in their life.

"He doesn't want your pity, Olivia, and maybe that's why he's said nothing to you." Bob stopped for a moment for breath. "He's lonely, Olivia. Aside from the fact the two of you were meant to be together, he needs you."

Belated understanding flashed in her blue eyes. "You planned all this. You purposely searched him out and asked him to be your doctor to bring us together."

"Regretful men have to make amends, do the right thing to find the peace they're looking for before death. But it wasn't all noble, Olivia. George is one of the best in his field."

"He is that, but still, you concocted all this. You sought George and me out to bring us together."

"Would it be a bad thing if I did?" Bob said with a faint smile.

Olivia shook her head.

"You know, Olivia, I smell a best-selling book in our story," Bob said with a wink and another faint smile when he read the exciting realization in her eyes.

Olivia was overdosing on excitement for a woman who'd experienced little in her life.

Epilogue

HIS PEACE MADE with Olivia and the loose ends tied, the following day, with his daughter, his wife, his doctor, Lottie, Bonita, Rose, and Oreo by his side, at the age of fifty-five, Bob drifted into his permanent sleep.

His last words were, "You will forever be among the greatest thing to happen to me, Cassie. You're wonderful, and you make me wonderful. You, Cassie, made me the man I am today. My heart is full of you and will forever be. I love you."

There wasn't a dry eye in the room.

Olivia buried Bob next to her mother and father at the Holy Cross Cemetery. The stone on Bob's grave read: In life, we err; make amends, and are forgiven. I was forgiven and left memories worth remembering. I serenely rest.

"Those are beautiful words, Olivia." Cassie laid down the red rose on Bob's grave.

"I'm glad you like them." Olivia laid down her flower. "You can visit Bob as often as you like, Cassie."

Cassie mopped at the tears. "It's sad his sister and nephews didn't want to say goodbye."

The day was bright with sunshine. The flowers on Bob's grave and those surrounding him perfumed the air. Olivia heard Oreo's bark in the distance as Lottie, Rose, Bonita, Sondra, Malcolm, and George walked to their cars to give her time with Cassie.

Olivia draped an arm over Cassie's shoulders. "They will when they're ready. Everyone mourns differently."

She lifted her shoulders, then let them fall. "I guess. When Mom died, there were so many people there. Neighbours, her boss, and friends from work came. Even some of the patients she cared for at the nursing home came."

"It sounds as if she was very much loved." Olivia's voice was full of warmth and sympathy.

"She was. When she got sick, we got behind on the bills, rent, electricity, and everything else. When she died, I ended up homeless. Mrs. Pyre, my mom's boss at the nursing home, took me in. She let me stay in one of the vacant rooms, and I worked for my keep. I cleaned the resident's rooms, did the clothes washing, fed them, and took them for walks, things like that. But I couldn't stay there forever. I was taking up an expensive room. That's when I decided to go look for Dad."

There were times Olivia wondered if there was a God. Cassie was a child, sixteen or seventeen when she lost her mother, her home, and the only life she knew. How fair was it to visit such pain and trauma on a young girl?

Olivia ran a hand over Cassie's hair. "That's very brave of you."

"Not brave. You do what you need to do, you know."

Olivia pulled Cassie closer. "Yeah, I know."

Cassie caught her bottom lip between her teeth and fell deep in thought. When she found the strength, she asked the question. "Can I stay with you for a while, Olivia?"

Olivia shook her head. "I'm sorry, Cassie."

"I won't be a burden. I'll work for my keep, you know. I'll clean the house. They taught me how to do that at the nursing home. I can cook while you finish your novel. Well, not really cook. I mean, I can make peanut butter and jelly sandwiches. I can make pasta sauce," Cassie added.

Olivia turned Cassie to face her and took hold of her shoulders. "I meant to say I'm sorry I didn't get a chance to tell you. My mind has been fogged with the funeral arrangements and everything going on. Bob asked me to take care of you, and I told him I'd be happy to. That is if you'd like to slum it with a woman who ditched a paying job to write a book, which won't pay anything for a long time. I have some savings, but it will be tight for a while and...."

"So, I'm staying with you and Oreo at your house?" Cassie jumped in excitedly.

"Yes, if you want."

"Yes, I want," Cassie said quickly, too quickly. "And don't worry about money. I have some that Daddy left me."

"That's your money, but don't worry, we'll manage, and when we can't, I'll figure something out."

"But...." Oreo's bark echoed, and Cassie glanced up as he came running across the green carpet of tended grass. Grinning, Cassie bent down and picked him up. "She said yes, Oreo. We're going to be roomies," she whispered in Oreo's ear, and he gave a happy bark and followed it with a doggy grin.

The beginning of one life and the end of another.

THERE WAS NO LIFE INSURANCE POLICY.

So typical of Bob, or so Olivia thought until reading his will. Olivia was the beneficiary of a fifteen-million-dollar inheritance Bob left, and the same went for Cassie.

The thirty million dollars was Bob's inheritance upon his mother's death, which she acquired through the sale of the law firm her husband built.

Law is a profitable business, Olivia thought.

It was safe to surmise the inheritance money was the reason Bob asked Olivia to protect Cassie from Michelle. Knowing Michelle, as Olivia did, she resented Bob for getting such a large piece of the family pie.

Unlike Bob, Michelle didn't abandon the family. She stayed and fulfilled the role of the perfect daughter Robert James Huntley Sr. demanded. Although she detested the field of law, Michelle became a lawyer to please her father. She married Jackson Knut, a partner at the firm, to please daddy. Huntley's blood ran through her two boys, bred to carry the Huntley legacy.

By Michelle's reasoning, she, her children, and her husband deserved every dime of her mother's estate. She deserved to inherit the firm. Her mother had no right to sell her share and hand the money to Bob. Bob didn't earn a dime and didn't deserve it. Besides, he'd only squander it as he had his life.

Olivia shelved the thought that, in time, she'd have to deal with Michelle and focused on the now. She and Cassie moved into the Huntley Estate, a sprawling twenty acres of rolling green north of the city. The Georgian-style home was as grand in stature as it was in history. It had been under Huntley's ownership for generations, but it now belonged to Cassie, a non-Huntley.

White, tall pilasters flanked the home's arched entrance with many large picture windows. Lush, colourful gardens hemmed the house. A cobbled road lined with red maples and lampposts wound into a circular driveway. A gurgling brook ran through the property with a paddock and stable with horses, a swimming pool, and an extended deck overlooking the rolling hills dotted with elms, maples, and firs. Oreo was in heaven.

As spectacular as the property was, at Olivia's time of life, familiar and cozy suited her better. She would rather have stayed in her small two-story red brick home. Cassie, however, felt close to Bob at the estate. It was his childhood home, where they'd spent the last three years, and at a time like this, Cassie's well-being trumped Olivia's.

When Cassie was ready, she enrolled at the local high school. Her goal was to get her diploma and pursue her dream of becoming a nurse. As Rose and Bonita did for Bob, taking care of people during their last days of life was Cassie's goal.

Olivia dug her heels into her writing. Her creativity flourished, and writing no longer felt like a chore but her life's ambition. She breathed and lived writing. Olivia felt as if she had awakened from a dream that sprung to life. It was a long time since her life was on track.

There was no stopping Olivia. Before she knew it, summer slid into fall and fall into winter, and her story for *The Fearless Woman* evolved into the novel she had in her for so long but couldn't articulate until now.

Maybe it was the peaceful, rural surroundings of Huntley Estate. No doubt, the stress-free days contributed to her creativity. The anger and bitterness brought on during her time at Sullivan's, now left behind, made her creative. But mainly, Olivia attributed her newfound creativity to the blossoming relationship between her and George.

The schedule of an oncologist was demanding, but George made time for Olivia. They spent all of their spare time together, but seven months in, she hadn't crossed that line as much as she wanted him in her bed. Regardless of his wife's mental debilitation, he was a married man.

"So, Cassie tells me you're almost finished with your book." George's eyes followed Olivia to the bar and watched her pour whiskey for him and a glass of red wine for her.

Her chestnut hair fountained her face. She wore a lilac shirt open at the neck, blue jeans, and fuzzy pink slippers. She smelled gently of sweet perfume.

"It's only the first draft," she said.

George took the offered glass and knocked part of the whiskey back. He felt it loosen the week's stress away. "It's not an only. It's a great accomplishment. You should be proud of yourself," he said, stroking Oreo's head.

Olivia dropped the needle on the record, and Sade sensually crooning By Your Side came to life. The music, the cozy warmth in the room from the crackling fire in the hearth, and the serene view of falling snow out the living room window lent a romantic feel to the moment.

Olivia sat on the long, cream-coloured leather couch next to George. Shedding her fuzzy slippers, she tucked her legs under her. "I am proud. It's been a long time coming, but it's just the beginning. There are several edits it will undergo before I'm fully pleased." Her eyes on George, she took a sip of wine.

Tonight he looked particularly handsome, she thought. His snow-damp hair glistened under the lights. He wore a gray suit against a powder blue silk shirt and cobalt tie. The day's stubble looked good on him.

He put a nice cozy fire in her stomach. It had been long since a man stirred her insides as George did.

"I can read it for you and edit it if you like." He watched her brows form that uncertain crease between them he knew well. "Only a suggestion. I know how guarded authors are of their writing."

"I'm not an author. I'm a writer, fulfilling a dream."

His hand closed over hers. "The offer is there for you when you're ready," he said, and she understood the meaning of the words went beyond editing. "Where's Cassie?"

"She's out on a date." Olivia took his glass to refill it.

Oreo jumped off the couch when Olivia rose, walked to the fireplace, and spread out on the shag carpet. Before the crackle of flame and wood, belly up, he fell asleep.

"It's been a rough day for him?" George said.

"Eating, sleeping, and barking at squirrels can take a toll on you." She refreshed George's glass with Jack Daniel's.

"It's about time Cassie got herself a life. Did you give the boy an eye over?" George broke into a smile when Oreo's snores came loud.

"I did. He's a nice young man she met during her volunteer rounds at the hospital, but you knew that already since you introduced him to her."

"I hope you don't mind. I thought they'd be good for each other, and I had the fatherly talk with him."

"Good, it never hurts to have a man's input. And I know you have Cassie's best interest at heart."

"He's a rising oncologist under my expert tutelage."

There was humour in George's eyes still, her eyebrows winged. "Hopefully, he's impervious to your modesty."

Grinning, George reached for the glass Olivia held out. "Have you told Cassie about the email you received from Michelle threatening to contest your inheritances?"

Olivia shook her head. "I'll deal with Michelle myself. There's no need for Cassie to know the woman she considers her aunt is out to hurt her," she responded in defence and defiance. "Cassie is still getting past Bob's death and getting her life together, and I don't want to inject such ugliness into her recovery. If Michelle wants a fight, I say, bring it on. I'm up for it." Olivia took a long sip of wine to numb the sickness in her belly the topic brought on. "I don't understand why Michelle needs to do this. I know Cassie, and I got a lot of money, but she got a very profitable firm worth far more than what she paid her mother for her share."

"She's not doing it for the money. She's doing it for spite and to expose Cassie's not a Huntley."

Olivia felt her stomach lurch. The thought of Cassie's life being upended again by Michelle's vindictiveness was unnecessary and deplorable. Cassie had had more than her share of heartbreak at her young age and didn't deserve any additional grief at this time. She was still healing.

"I'd give Michelle every last dime of my inheritance, but it wouldn't satisfy her. She's hell-bent on hurting Cassie." She walked across the room and set her eyes out the window.

The moon sat high in the sky. The snow, falling in thick, listless sheets, covered everything under a thick white layer. The driveway lampposts shone light onto the snow, making it gleam white, a sharp contrast against the dark sky. Olivia heard the howling wind beat against the windowpane.

George rose and walked to her. "I'm in your corner, Livy. I'll support you, whatever you decide to do. I'll even help you fight Michelle if that's what you want to do."

She met his eyes in the reflection on the window. "You will."

George nodded. "I want to be a part of your life, Livy." He spun her around so they were face to face. "I want to be there for you, with you every step. Would you like that?"

She nodded.

"Good. You will need me by your side when your book is published." She gave him a puzzled look. "Cassie tells me…."

"I'm starting to think Cassie talks too much."

He had to smile at that. "What can I say? I'm easy to talk to."

"Or too probing."

There was the sharp tongue of the Livy he knew. The smile morphed into a smirk. "When your book gets published, connections will be made, and heads will roll. Yours may be one of them."

Now her grin flashed. "This is a work of fiction. Names, characters, and incidents are the product of the author's imagination and are used fictitiously. Any resemblance to actual persons, living or crushed by greed, is entirely coincidental," she recited in an uninflected voice.

"You added the 'crushed by greed' part, right? I'm not a lawyer, but that didn't sound like legal jargon." At her nod, his lips stretched out in a smile. "So, we're in this great big house alone." George ran his fingers through her hair and made the unabashed arousal assault her and stir her insides.

"Except for Sondra and Malcolm, who finished moving into the guesthouse today, we're alone."

"Boundaries have been laid out?"

"Yes, Sondra, whom Cassie, as part of her pay-it-forward mission, invited to live here free of charge, has gone over her rules with us in extensive detail." George's laughter was a rich male sound she liked. "Anyway, those two are too busy to…. Yes, we're alone," she finished.

"I hoped you'd say that." Tempting fate, he chained his arms around her and was pleased when she let him.

His scent, strong and masculine, slid into her and her stomach lurched in a good way this time. A very good way, she thought and leaned into him. His chest was solid and as comforting as a down pillow.

God, she wanted so much more than to breathe his familiar scent. She wanted fire, the type he'd ignite in her. Maybe they could come back whole from a night together to watch the dawn of a new day.

The soulful sound of Otis Redding's voice singing I've Been Loving You Too Long flowed from the record player.

"Dance with me, Livy." George reached for her hand and pulled her tight to him before she could refuse. "My love is growing stronger as you become a habit to me." He spun her around the room and sang with Otis.

Olivia felt as if she was floating on a cloud. "You know the lyrics by heart."

"I do. It's our song," he said.

"We have a song?"

He nodded and jumped in to sing with Otis. "With you, my life has been so wonderful."

He had gentle hands that touched her with feeling and warmth. She felt his warm breath against her neck. It felt so very good to her.

Drifting with Otis, they glided around the room. "Take me to your bed, Livy."

Those cerulean eyes met his eyes, and in them, she saw desire in the brandy-coloured eyes. "You're married, George."

"I want to make love with you, Livy. I want to kiss you, touch you, and explore your body. I want to hear you moan my name. I want to whisper yours in your ear." He felt her melt in his arms just as he wanted her to.

Sweet and sour, Jesus. Too tempted to walk him upstairs, she tried pulling away, but he held her tighter.

"I am married, but only on paper, Livy. We haven't been a married couple in a long time, but I can't abandon her right now. Her mind is too fragile to deal with the idea of divorce. Can you understand that?"

Olivia said nothing.

She understood, she even found his sense of duty admirable, but it didn't feel right to take the husband of an ill woman to bed. She'd told him as much every time they came close to crossing the line.

"My children understand my need to move on and have encouraged it."

"You talked to your kids about me?"

He nodded. "It's taken all these months to muster the courage, but I finally did and talked to them about us. It's important to me to have their blessing. I couldn't have them hating you or me. Can you understand that?" She nodded. "To my surprise, I've stressed all these months for no reason. They wondered why I hadn't moved on sooner." He drew her back far enough to look into her eyes.

"I want to make a life with you, Livy, and Cassie. I want to wake up with you next to me. I want to come home to you and talk about my day. I want you to be a part of my life. Bob gave us this chance to come together and compensate for lost time, and I need to take it. I don't want to lose you again. I know I come with a lot of baggage, and I'll walk away if you want me to, Livy. No questions asked." He tucked a stray strand of her hair behind her ear. "But know this, Livy. I love you. I always have. I'm sorry I didn't say it sooner."

There was silence, one long beat before Olivia brushed her lips to his tenderly. "I love you, George," she said and reached for his hand.

There's no past anymore. There's only the now.

Sneak peek at M.L. Lexi's new novel

THE LOYAL WOMAN

One

Monday, September 7, Morning

SOLEDAD THOMAS STARTED her ordinary day by making breakfast for her family, something she had done on hundreds of Mondays. However, today, her day would turn from ordinary to the worst.

White cupboards and tan quartz countertops gleamed under the September sunshine pouring bright through the windows. The smell of frying bacon, scrambled eggs, and toast painted the air. Monday's breakfast menu was always bacon, scrambled eggs, and toast. Consistency was of the utmost importance to Elliot and what he expected of his wife.

Breakfast finished, and the family was off to their busy lives. Elliot was off to carry out his COO duties at Thomas and Partners, his father's accounting firm. The twins, Allie and Annie, and Soledad's youngest, Noah, were off to school to fill their minds with knowledge and teenage angst.

As Soledad did every morning, she watched everyone pile into Elliot's Maserati from the living room window. The usual routine played out precisely as it did every morning. The twins opened the back car doors, always

Allie on the right and Annie on the left. Always toss backpacks in, slide into the seats, snap seatbelts in, and set the AirPods in their ears, proceed with head bobbing to the music. Noah got into the front passenger seat, and Elliot behind the wheel. Off they went at eight-fifteen. Always at eight-fifteen. Elliot would drop the children off at school at eight twenty-five, and he would be in his office by eight fifty-five. Always.

Monotony and repetitiveness had become Soledad's life, and Christ, she hated the feeling of boredom and predictability that was her life.

Her family wasn't tedious, her children anything but monotone. Soledad loved her children and husband, and she loved who they were. Or did she?

Doubt had become the essence of her being.

When Elliot turned right on Maple, and the car disappeared, on a long, exhaled breath, Soledad swirled from the window and got on with her humdrum Monday. She had a long list of chores to get to.

First on the day's schedule was laundry, and in the laundry room, Soledad separated, sorted, and tossed the first of many loads she'd do that morning into the washing machine. There was never a shortage of dirty laundry with three fashion-conscious teenagers and a husband.

Soledad was glad Hope and Jasmine, her two eldest, no longer lived at home. As much as Soledad missed them, she was glad they'd moved out when they started university and that independent living stuck after graduation. Two fewer bodies at home took off some of the pressure from her hectic days.

Since birth, Soledad cared for her five children on her own. There had been no nannies, babysitters, or family support. There was no help of any kind. It hadn't been easy. At times, it had been stressful. It was often taxing on the body and mind, but Soledad had done it.

Elliot was the professional, the educated one, the breadwinner. Soledad was the stay-at-home mom, and her job was to care for the children and home and organize her family's lives. Soledad had sacrificed her life to meet their needs. She'd done her part for the past thirty-one years to meet her family's needs and make them happy— at the cost of her happiness.

As much as Soledad loved her children and enjoyed being a mother and wife, her resentment was ready to burst.

Soledad told herself every married woman went through the existential crisis she was going through, and it would pass. It hadn't. The emptiness and disillusion with her life were mounting to distraction, and she feared what she might do. Everyone had a breaking point.

Adding detergent, Soledad turned the dial and set the machine to wash. Her lips curved when Buddy's head spun in chorus with the spin cycle swirling through the glass window. The silly-looking, brown pug with deep wrinkles around the big, dark eyes always put a smile on her face no matter her mood, and this morning's mood was sad and broody.

Today was Soledad's fiftieth birthday, a day she'd dreaded for weeks.

She'd cruised past twenty into thirty without much thought. Her mind was occupied then with marriage and children. She'd inched her way into forty with a hope and a prayer her fiftieth wouldn't come anytime soon. Yet here was her fiftieth birthday, sooner than expected and adding to her feelings of hopelessness.

Soledad hated feeling as she did about a silly birthday, but it was her fiftieth—the worst number in her books.

The big five-oh was the crossover into old age, the time you re-evaluate your life and doubt your choices. It brought on menopause, giving rise to gray hair and hot flashes, a constant reminder of your ageing body. The five-oh brought on dormant disorders and pain you never imagined would touch you. Worse, fifty brought on drooping boobs, the horrors of the turkey neck, and sagging arms, sagging everything.

Soledad's mood was somewhat lifted by the idea of her family coming home tonight. She didn't doubt they would all make it home to surprise her. It was why no one had mentioned her birthday at the breakfast table.

Elliot would show up with a chocolate-chip ice cream cake, the family's favourite and a bouquet of roses. Noah would present her with a bundle of variety-store bought flowers. Hope and Jasmine would override their father's set menu and order Chinese and pizza, and the entire family would gather around the dining room table.

Tonight though, Soledad decided there would be no fast food. With everyone's life going in different directions, it was a rare occasion when her family shared family dinner together, and Soledad planned to make it memorable. She planned to prepare a grand dinner with everyone's favourite foods.

Right now, though, it was time for Buddy's morning walk. The last thing she wanted was a present from Buddy scenting the house.

Walking to the foyer, Soledad looked at herself in the closet door mirror. Her chestnut hair was bound into a messy ponytail. Black leggings designed to smooth out her long legs were paired with a short sleeve Lycra shirt that tightly hugged her body and gave her feminine curves. Except for the gold wedding band on her left hand, she wore no jewellery. She wasn't June Cleaver, and jewelry and housework weren't an ideal match. The same went for makeup, but she needed none. The long, lashed blue eyes, the dainty nose, and delicate pouty mouth on the alabaster face needed no enhancements.

Soledad reached for her pear-yellow running jacket. She slipped on her white running shoes and strapped the running belt that held her water bottle and cell phone around her waist.

Eyeing herself in the mirror, Soledad looked every bit the runner. Too bad she didn't run, hadn't since Hope, her firstborn, came along. Women her age who were mothers and wives, managers of their homes, ran in the movies and fiction novels. Women who were their husband's caterers and hosted the many functions to promote their scaling careers didn't have time to run.

Soledad eyed her screen's phone for the time. Eight-thirty, time for Buddy's half-hour morning walk. Elliot's motto was that schedules made for an efficient life, and he was a stickler for efficiency.

"Buddy, can you pull yourself away from watching the washing to go for your morning walk?" Soledad smiled when Buddy made a mad dash from the laundry room and slid across the polished hardwood and into her. "I thought that would get your attention. Let's get going. We have exactly thirty minutes for your walk. I have a lot to do today." She attached Buddy's leash to his collar as his tail happily thumped against hardwood.

Coming Soon

The Complete Woman
The Conflicted Woman
The Spiteful Woman
The Tortured Woman

The Relentless Woman Duology

The Relentless Woman
The Vindictive Women

The Unbreakable Woman Trilogy

The Unbreakable Woman
The Brave Woman
The Valiant Woman

Contact us

Email us at mllexiauthor@gmail.com to receive emails whenever M.L. Lexi publishes a new book. There is no charge or obligation and your information will remain confidential.

Visit us at www.mllexi.com to read excerpts of upcoming releases.